The Fear

'[These stories] evoke a sense of wonder at the mystery and beauty of creation and invite reflection on the cycle of life, death and renewal in nature, and the nature of being and reality. The stories are however sufficiently grounded in a child's world to hold the attention of all but the most worldly of 8–12 year olds... The metaphysical element elevates the book above the common-place.'

Books for Keeps

'Wangerin's prose appears to draw on folktale for its allegorical structures and the magic realist school for its gleaming lyricism, and the result is a text that fairly shimmers with allusion and music.'

Literacy and Learning

Walter Wangerin, Jr has written award-winning books for both children and adults, including the bestsellers *The Book of God* and *The Book of the Dun Cow*. In the United States he is a well-known speaker and storyteller, radio host and writer-in-residence at Valparaiso University, Indiana. An ordained Lutheran minister, Walter Wangerin served as pastor of an inner-city church for 15 years. He and his wife Ruthanne have four children and live in Indiana.

The Fear Not Angel

WALTER WANGERIN, JR

LION
Children's Books

Published by
Lion Publishing plc
Sandy Lane West, Oxford, England
www.lion-publishing.co.uk
ISBN 0 7459 4045 5

First hardback edition 1998
First paperback edition 1999
10 9 8 7 6 5 4 3 2 1 0

Acknowledgments
Potter first published in 1985 by Chariot Books, USA.
Branta and the Golden Stone first published in 1993 by
Simon & Schuster Books for Young Readers, USA.
Thistle first published in 1995 by Augsburg Fortress, USA.
Probity Jones and the Fear Not Angel first published in 1996
by Augsburg Fortress, USA.

Published in association with the literary agency
of Alive Communications, 1465 Kelly Johnson Blvd.,
Suite 320, Colorado Springs, Colorado 80920, USA.

Cover illustration reproduced from *Probity Jones and the Fear
Not Angel* by Walter Wangerin Jr., illustrated by Tim Ladwig,
copyright © 1996 Augsburg Fortress. Used by permission.

A catalogue record for this book is available
from the British Library

Printed and bound in Great Britain by
Cox & Wyman, Reading

Contents

Probity Jones
and the
Fear Not Angel

*T*he whole family was getting dressed to go out—everyone except Probity. Probity Jones was sick. Her mother had told her she was too sick to leave the apartment tonight.

'I'm sorry child,' her mother had said. 'You're burnin' with fever, and it's colder than zero outside.'

'Oh, Mama, I *got* to go,' Probity begged, trying to sit up. 'I been plannin' this for weeks. I memorized all the words. I can say them perfectly. Please, Mama—please let me go with you.'

Then her mother heaved a sorrowful sigh. It was the kind of sigh that always made Probity feel bad. Her mother was worn out from working, worn out from taking care of her four children alone, worn out from being forever and ever poor. How could Probity argue with such a sigh?

'Baby,' her mother said, 'when I lost your daddy to sickness, I promised God I'd never lose another soul. I'm keeping the family whole and you are staying home tonight.'

So that was final.

And now Probity could hear her sisters laughing in the kitchen.

'Snip-snip! Snip-snip!' That was Elfrieda. 'Snip the tinfoil, make a star, and cover it over with glitter!'

Probity lay on the sofa in the front room. It was dark outside. Probity was watching the white moon through the window. It shined on the snowy tops of the evergreen trees, but it moved all alone in heaven. Probity thought, *The moon is as lonely as I am.*

8

Just then her little brother started to yell, 'Where's my baffrobe? Who stole my baffrobe? I can't go without my baffrobe, you know!'

Elfrieda said, 'Go ask Probity. Girls who lose expensive coats are liable to steal bathrobes too.'

The kitchen door burst open. Light rushed into the front room. So did Probity's brother with his lip stuck out.

'Probity!' He marched to the sofa and gave her a punch on the shoulder. 'Did you steal my baffrobe to wear to church tonight on account of you lost your own coat?'

'No, Charles.' Probity felt like crying. 'I don't have your bathrobe, and I'm not going with you tonight.'

Charles' eyes grew large. 'Why not?' he said. He grabbed his sister's nightgown. 'Probity, you *got* to go!'

'I can't,' she said.

' 'Cause you lost your coat? 'Cause Mama's mad at you? You can wear my baffrobe. I don't mind.'

'No, Charles. It's because I'm sick.'

Her little brother got tears in his eyes. 'But I'm scared without you, Probe,' he said. 'You and me, we're supposed to say the words *together*. How can I say the words without you?'

Probity touched his cheek and said, 'Say them now.'

Charles frowned. He said, 'Let us go—' He paused and frowned harder. 'Let us go now— Let us now go—' Then he wailed, 'Oh, Probity, I don't know it. I can't say it without you!'

'Shhh,' said Probity, 'Listen to me: *Let us now go even unto Bethlehem*—'

9

But Charles only howled louder and tried to pull his sister off the sofa. 'I need you, Probe. I really need you!'

Then their mother came into the room with a wrinkled cotton bathrobe. 'Baby brother, you're gon' lay me in my grave,' she sighed. 'Take this and dress your sorry self. Hurry! We leave in two minutes.'

Charles ran from the room yelling, 'I'm going to mess up! Nobody cares if I mess up!'

Probity's mother gazed at her a while. 'I'm not mad at you for losing the coat,' she said. 'I'm just worried. I don't know how to get you another one.' She leaned down and kissed her daughter in the middle of the forehead. 'Mrs Johnson down on the second floor—she knows you're home. I asked her to look in on you. Get well, little sister. I love you. I do.'

It was Christmas Eve. Tonight the children were going to church to be in the Christmas pageant. Charles and Carolyn and Elfrieda were supposed to be shepherds. Charles had the speaking part—and Probity had been picked to be the Fear Not Angel, the best part she ever had in her life. She had memorized the words: *Behold, I bring you good tidings of great joy...*

But her mother was right. She was very sick. Probity's bones ached, her brains felt woozy, she was sweaty-cold all over.

Now Elfrieda popped into the front room and shined a flashlight on her grinning face. 'See the sparkles?' she said.

Sure enough: Probity saw tiny twinklings of glitter in her sister's hair.

Elfrieda waved a stick that had a tinfoil star at the end of it, also covered with glitter. 'My invention,' she said. 'This is the star the wise men follow to Bethlehem. Everyone says it's a good thing you messed up, Probe. I'll make a better angel than you. I know how to dress pretty—and I don't lose my clothes. Bye!'

The kitchen light went off. The back door opened and shut. Then the whole family clattered down the apartment stairs, past Mrs Johnson's place on the second floor, past the Alvarez's on the first, and out into the snow.

Probity could hear them laughing as they walked off to church.

She stared at the moon, perfectly round in the lonely sky, perfectly white. Glitter sparkled in the darkness. Ten million stars, ten million bits of ice. Probity Jones felt miserable.

She began to shiver. No matter how many blankets covered her, she felt as if she were outside without a coat.

And that, of course, is exactly what had happened to her yesterday.

School had let out early for the Christmas holidays, and Probity Jones was walking home through a dangerous neighbourhood. She should not have gone alone. And she surely should not have been wearing her new coat. She had spent the whole morning showing it off to everyone in school.

At twelve noon it started to snow.

Then three boys began to follow her. So Probity made her feet go faster.

'Wait! Wait!' the boys hollered. 'We just wanna talk.'

Probity clutched her schoolbag and ran as fast as she could.

They ran too, smooth as athletes, laughing and calling, 'Give it up, girl! We the marathon men! Ain' no one can escape from us!'

The snow was falling harder now. Probity cut down a narrow alley and kept on running until she heard nothing but her own steps. She stopped. She stood still, holding her breath, listening. The snow was like curtains.

But suddenly two boys appeared behind her and one in front, yelling, 'Where you think you goin', girl?'

'Home,' said Probity Jones. 'I'm going home.'

The loud boy grabbed her bag and opened it. 'How you plannin' to *get* home?' he sneered.

'Walking,' said Probity. She felt like she would cry soon. 'Give me back my bag!'

The boy pulled out her papers and threw them into the wind, then pushed the empty bag against her stomach. 'No, no, you don't understand,' he growled. 'How you plan to *pay* to get home?'

'Pay?' Probity whispered. 'Pay? I don't have anything.'

The boy stood back and roared, 'Now you are a liar for sure! We saw you sashayin' all up and *down* the school hall, proud of that coat. The coat, girl! The coat is our pay. Give us your coat and you can go.'

Her new coat! Probity could not take it off. She could only bow her head and cry.

So the boys unzipped the expensive coat. They held her arms back and pulled off the sleeves, then vanished in the whirling snowfall.

The wind was howling. All the city was hidden in white. Probity wore nothing but jeans and a cotton shirt, and now she was lost. It must have been after two o'clock when she found her way home, shaking with cold and very sick.

Knock, knock!

So now it was Christmas Eve. And Probity lay in the front room shivering and sweaty, both at once. Even the moon was gone now. Outside and inside, the whole world was lonely, dark, and cold.

Knock, knock.

Probity thought she heard someone knocking in the apartment.

Knock, knock.

There it was again. Poor Probity! Even under the covers she was freezing. But maybe it was Mrs Johnson, come to check on her. So the child slipped the blankets aside and put her bare feet down on the wooden floor. She started to walk to the kitchen door, but: *Knock, knock, knock!* The knocking was right here in the front room! *Knock, knock!*—the window! Someone was knocking on the outside of the window!

Probity crept over to the window and saw that the snow had begun to fall again, as thick as wool and perfectly quiet.

But then in the midst of the snow she saw something else. She gasped. Just outside the window was a beautiful person dressed all in white as bright as the moon, looking straight back into Probity's eyes.

This person smiled, then opened the window on the tips of her fingers and said, *Come, Probity Jones. It's time to go.*

Probity could only stare. *Go where?* she whispered.

The person outside was as tall as the night. She had wings wider than the dawn with feathers more silent than snow. Her robes were silken, and over her shoulders she wore a shawl of the softest cashmere.

She bent down and kissed Probity in the centre of her forehead. *Why, to the Christmas Pageant, of course*, she said.

The beautiful person reached through the window and gathered Probity up in her arms. She breathed on the child from her head to her toes, and Probity grew warm.

The thick snow surrounded them, and the apartment building was swallowed up, and it seemed that they were flying.

Yes, yes! They soared so high in the night that the city and all the falling snow went down below them.

They ascended to the pathways of the moon, where the night is kind and ten million stars are the sizes of children, and everyone was flying eastward, eastward.

But then Probity glanced down and saw white mountain peaks below her bare feet. She started to whimper, *Oh, no! Oh, no!*

But the one who carried her said, *Fear not, Probity. God would never let you fall—and who else but God has invited you to the pageant?*

They crossed a sea as deep as dreaming, then they began to descend over another country, a dark one, a land where the only light was fires. Campfires, cook fires, torches. Probity saw round hills in the night, narrow gorges between them, and little villages made out of wood and stone.

Faster and faster the hills rose up. They seemed covered with snow.

No, not snow! The white on the hills was wool! Sheep's wool. Probity was looking at sheep asleep on the hillside— and there beside them were shepherds too, three shepherds keeping watch over the flocks.

Hush now, whispered the person who had flown so far, so swift and silently with Probity. *Hide inside my shawl, child—and watch. Watch.*

Lower they sailed to the shepherds on wings as wide as the wind. Brighter and brighter the beautiful person began to shine, until the light on the hillside was more glorious than the sun—and all at once Probity knew who this was. This grand and shining figure was the Fear Not Angel!

The poor shepherds were terrified by the brightness. They dropped to the ground and covered their heads with their arms.

But the angel said, *Fear not. Behold, I bring you good tidings of great joy—*

Wait! Probity knew these words! These were the very words she had memorized for the pageant. Oh, she was happy now! She stuck her head out beneath the angel's throat and sang along as loudly as she could sing. She and the angel sang together:

For unto you is born this day in the city of David a Saviour, which is Christ the Lord!

The shepherds lowered their arms and looked up. Two of them had glitter in their hair. One was wearing an old wrinkled bathrobe.

Probity and the angel sang: *And this shall be a sign unto you.
Ye shall find the babe wrapped in swaddling clothes, lying in a manger.*

Suddenly all the stars in heaven flew down, ten million
angels the sizes of children. It was as if the whole sky were a
great wheel turning and burning: the angels circled the hills
and the night and the shepherds, singing, *Glory to God in the
highest, and peace to the people with whom he is pleased!*

The shepherds leaped up and raised their hands,
worshipping God.

And when the roaring chorus was over and the hosts had
flown back into heaven and the Fear Not Angel, too, had
dimmed her brightness, Probity saw that two of the shepherds
were smiling. But one was frowning, the one with the wrinkled
bathrobe. Her heart was beating hard for that shepherd.

He coughed. He rubbed his forehead. He muttered, *Let us
now... go... even—* Suddenly he threw back his head and
shouted at the top of his lungs: *Go even unto Bethlehem, and see this
thing which is come to pass, which the Lord hath made known unto us!*

Probity clapped her hands. She clapped and clapped and
wished that she could kiss the little shepherd, but no one
heard her, and all three shepherds were already racing over
the hills to the north.

Once more the Fear Not Angel rose up, carrying Probity
still in her shawl of cashmere. They flew north until they
stopped above a little village, directly over a little stable.

It started to snow—a light fall of sparkling snow. Probity
saw the shepherds rushing through the village to the stable

below. There they bent down and crept in through a low door. A lantern was burning inside.

Then she noticed three men coming from the opposite direction, big men, strange and strong. They were pointing up at Probity as if she had something important for them, and immediately Probity knew what they needed. They needed a holy light to show them where the baby king was. These were the wise men searching for Christ the Lord!

So Probity whispered in the ear of the Fear Not Angel, *Please, can we go down some? And can I shine like you for a while?*

The Fear Not Angel descended through the snow, then set Probity upon the air right over the door of the stable. *Probity Jones, I'm going to miss you*, said the Angel. She removed the fine white shawl of cashmere and wrapped it around the child. *This shall be your shining*, she said. *This shall be your light.*

The Angel vanished in thick snow, leaving Probity and her shawl shining as bright as any star.

So the wise men were able to see through the blizzard. They followed Probity's radiance until they came to the door of the stable. *That's the one*, they said, *the star we followed from the east!*

Then the wise men too, like the shepherds, bowed their heads and entered the stable to worship the king.

Now it was Probity's turn.

She wrapped the fine white shawl around herself and walked down the air as if it were steps. She knew what everyone was looking at inside the stable, for hadn't she told the shepherds the news? And hadn't she led the wise men here? Yes: they were looking at the Virgin Mary, and at

Joseph standing beside her. And there, wrapped in a white cloth, lying in a manger, the beautiful child, the Christ, the king of creation. Dear little Jesus had been born tonight!

Probity went forward, prepared to go through the stable door. But the wind howled louder, and the snow blinded her. It swallowed the stable in whiteness. The girl bent her head against the screaming wind. She felt for the sides of the doorway. She grabbed them in her two hands, then put one foot through—though it was so dark inside that she couldn't see anything. Probity drew her other foot in, and suddenly the wind stopped blowing. It was quiet inside but perfectly dark.

Knock, knock.

Where were the shepherds and the wise men? Where was the baby Jesus? *Knock, knock!*

Someone was knocking far away. Someone else wanted to come in. Probity began to feel her way through the darkness toward the knocking—and she bumped into her old sofa, all the covers in a mess. *Knock, knock, knock!* Now she walked on the wooden floor to a door, to the kitchen door.

'Probity! Probity!' That was her little brother Charles' voice.

So Probity Jones switched on the light and ran to the back door of the apartment. She unlocked the lock, took hold of the doorknob and threw the door wide open.

Charles ran straight into the room and grabbed his sister and danced and danced. 'I did it! I did it!' he cried. 'I said all the words. Oh, Probe, it was just as if you were there with me!'

Elfrieda and Carolyn came in with snow-glitter on their

shoulders. 'Girl, you should've heard that angel sing,' they said. 'It was the angel of heaven. It surely was.'

But behind them all, still framed in the doorway, was Probity's mama, her eyes as bright as diamonds. She was staring hard at her daughter.

'Child, something happened here, didn't it?'

'Yes'm, it did,' Probity said.

'Look at you, baby. Look at my girl in a bright new coat!'

Probity walked forward and pressed her head against her mama's stomach.

The woman knelt down and hugged her. 'What, child?' she whispered. 'What happened tonight?'

'Oh mama, the angel of the Lord came down and carried me off to Bethlehem, and Jesus was born, and I was there, and so was Charles talkin' so beautiful—and Elfrieda and Carolyn, too. And I got to tell the good news to the people. Me, Mama! Probity Jones—I was at the pageant! We were all there together!'

Probity wrapped the shining shawl around her Mama and herself.

'And this came from the Fear Not Angel,' she said. 'Oh, Mama, the angel gave me a piece of herself to keep forever and forevermore.'

Lily

*O*nce upon a time—just last summer when the sun was warm and the leaves and the breezes were happy—three sisters lived at the edge of a northern forest: the oldest was named Bean Plant; the second sister, Marigold; and the youngest of all they called Lily.

Bean Plant was plain. Her flowers in June were tiny purses, white and very plain. Oh, but she worked! She worked. She opened her leaves and caught the sunlight—and by July she was growing green beans as long as sausages.

'Food,' said Bean Plant. 'Someone who feeds the birds and the squirrels is very important, don't you know.'

Marigold, the second sister, was beautiful. She said, 'Hum' and 'Oh, yes' and 'To be sure—I am a knock-out for prettiness!'

By August Marigold had put on such golden, glorious petals that she shined like the sun.

Did I say *like* the sun? Well, to tell you the truth, Marigold thought she was *better* than that big light in the sky, and that it was made to shine on *her*, so pretty and pretty was she!

Beautiful Marigold and busy Bean Plant—they had good friends and good reputations. The leaves and the breezes danced with them. The birds and the squirrels came to dinner. Almost everything in their lives was rich and good. Everything except their little sister.

'Shut up!' they said. 'Lily, Lily, either shut up or go away. You are embarrassing us!'

Lily had no blossom. One green stem a little too thick, and flat green leaves a little too weak, was Lily. She had no craft, and she had no beauty. But these things didn't bother her sisters. That's not why they shouted, 'Shut up! Shut up!'

Lily talked. All day long she talked. And always when she talked, she was talking to the *sun*!

Bean Plant said, 'The sun is fire and energy. It cannot talk!'

'Maybe not,' said Lily. 'And maybe so.'

Marigold said, 'The sun is a spotlight to shine on good things. Light-bulbs do not talk!'

'Maybe not,' said Lily. 'And maybe so.' She never argued with her sisters. But neither did she stop talking to the sun.

July and August and September: every morning when he rose in the east and leaned on the edge of the world, by his light alone the sun said, 'GOOD'.

Immediately Lily cried, 'Morning!'

And so they said, *Good morning* together.

Every noon, from highest heaven, the sun looked down and said, 'GOOD'.

And Lily on earth cried, 'Day!'

And so they said, *Good day* together.

And every evening, when the bloodred sun knelt on the western horizon, just before he went to bed, he whispered, 'GOOD'.

But then Lily never, never said, 'Bye'. She was scared of the word *Goodbye*, for she loved the sun and she wondered whether he loved her. She was waiting for the day when the sun would tell her that he loved her.

No, in the evening she always said, 'Night'.

And so they said, *Good night* together.

And Lily slept very well till the morning came again.

In October, Bean Plant and Marigold threw a party. They invited the birds and the squirrels and told them to bring their friends, too.

It was a wonderful party. Everyone talked about fur coats and feather hats and all the good food of the autumn.

The leaves put on their most colourful costumes.

And the breezes danced with Marigold. They swung her round and round until she could have died for joy.

But just after sunset, when the party was at its best, someone started to cry.

Did I say to *cry*? Oh, my, it was worse than that. She was shrieking. She was gasping and sobbing, boo-hooing and slobbering, bellowing, howling her sorrow.

Well, so that was the end of fun. Everyone felt gloomy, and the sister party-throwers were embarrassed to death.

'Lily! Lily!' Marigold screamed. 'Why are you crying?'

'Because of the sun,' poor Lily whispered.

'Yes? Yes?' Bean Plant snapped. 'And what *about* the sun?'

And Lily whispered, 'He's dying.'

'WHAT?' the sisters cried. 'THE SUN IS A FIRE! THE SUN IS A LIGHT! FIRES AND LIGHTS GO *OUT! THEY DO NOT DIE!*

But Lily said, 'Look how late he gets up in the morning now.'

The squirrels nodded. They agreed with this.

Lily said, 'Look how low he goes in the sky.'

The birds who flew admitted that this was true.

Lily said, 'And look how early he falls to bed. Every day the day grows colder. Every night the sun grows weaker.

He is dying. But he never yet told me,' Lily sobbed, 'that he loves me.'

'LOVES YOU?' screamed the sisters. This was crazy, crazy and humiliating. Not only was the party dead, but Lily was making their good friends nervous. The wind was chilly, and the leaves were shivering, for the sun indeed was declining.

Bean Plant said to them, 'Don't worry! Even if the sun should disappear, I can dry my beans and save the food for harder days!'

Marigold said, 'Don't worry! If that big light in the sky goes out, *I* will shine my lovely light for you.'

But time went by.

The sun grew weaker and weaker.

Lily met him day after day, again and again and again. She listened as she never had listened before. And in those days the dying sun taught her one more word, a powerful word, a promise word, a word to make poor Lily strong.

And then in grey November a new wind blew down from the north, a wind as white as ice and colder than the grave.

It tore all the leaves from the trees.

And as they fell to the ground, the dying leaves whispered a terrible message: *The killer! The killer! The killer is coming!*

Right away the birds took to their wings and flew south as fast as they could.

'We have to go!' they cried to the sisters. 'The killer is coming. No one, no one is safe! He kills,' called the birds as they vanished before the blinding white wind, 'the killer, he kills by kissing.'

Skinny Bean Plant now began to cry, 'It isn't fair! All my life I have worked *hard*. I've done my duty! I've been good! I don't deserve to die!'

Lily raised her voice and shouted, 'Bean Plant, don't worry! Everything will be right in the end. The sun has taught me one more word! He said...'

But Bean Plant cried, 'I want to live! I don't want to—'

And suddenly the oldest sister was perfectly silent, standing on one foot and quivering, because winter had kissed her, cold and mortal, as wooden as a broomstick in the middle of the field.

So Marigold started howling. 'But I'm so *beautiful!*' she bawled. 'I'm a treasure! I'm more golden than gold!'

Lily called to her, 'Don't worry, Marigold! Dying isn't so bad. The sun, he gave me the most important word...'

But poor Marigold felt the cold kiss coming. She screamed, 'I'm too beautiful to—' And in that instant the wind and the winter blasted her gold locks brown. Softly they sank to the ground.

And Lily, the youngest of all, was angry!

She glared straight into the wind and she scolded the winter: 'I hate you!' she shouted. 'I hate you for killing my sister Bean Plant, and my sister Marigold!'

Oh, Lily was strong now, that's the truth. She was not afraid. She was braver than daylight.

'And I hate you,' she shouted, 'for killing the bestest and the holiest thing of all, the sun, my sun, God's sun shining on the earth! Any time you want, old cold winter, just come and kiss me and see if I care!'

Well, and the winter did just that.

But Lily didn't cry.

Because the sun had taught her a word of perfect hope. Every day that the sun had returned to the morning, just by that returning alone, the sun had said: *Again.* That's the word. That's the promise that made Lily strong and not afraid: *Again, again, O Lily, I will come again.*

Now then, when spring returns this year to the edge of the northern forest where three sisters used to live, come with me. Let's go to the same place, too.

When we get there I will show you a fresh new lily—tall, a strong green stem, leaves like green hands, and a blossom as pure and white as the first light of the world.

You will look into that blossom and see a single drop of water trembling there.

You will say that it is a dew-drop.

But I will tell you the truth. It isn't dew at all. It is a tear-drop of perfect gladness.

For in spring the sun will come again. He will warm the earth and enter it to kiss the bulbs that lie below.

And this is how the sun will say, *I love you, Lily. Rise up and talk with me again, and we will make all of our days good forever and ever.*

And who could resist such loving and such life?

Not Lily.

Not me.

And I know this for a fact: not you.

Potter

*T*hree days, dear Jonathan. Three days is enough. Three days is too long for you to be gone. Come out! Come out! O Jonathan, come home again.

Potter knelt at the bedroom window, his elbows on the sill, his face in his hands, his eyes gone out to gaze over the yard and down the hill and to the woods at the bottom of that—and then the river. Adults were tramping the woods, but not Potter. Boats moved slowly upriver, and his own father was there, somewhere under the greening trees kicking last autumn's leaves, but not Potter. That was wrong.

Potter should have been looking for Jonathan the same as everyone else, because who was the best friend of Jonathan? Potter. And who knew all of the places where they hid the summer long: woven huts, stone fireplaces, secrets stored in bottles and metal boxes? Potter. Who knew the exact colour of Jonathan's red hair, and that he had white eyelashes and watery blue eyes and laughed like an ash can? Potter!

I could find you, Jonathan. I would say, Oh, there you are!

But Potter was not allowed to hunt for Jonathan. He knelt at the window, his forehead against the glass. Potter was not even allowed to leave the bedroom, and he should have been in bed, but he knelt at the window anyway. Potter was sick; he had a cough.

Winter always gave Potter this cough. He called it the Unstoppable Cough, and he plain got used to it, because what else could you do? The winter wind in Grand Forks,

North Dakota, came straight and hard. And it was a draughty old house they lived in, 619 Reeves Drive, two storeys. Through the weather, through the walls, through Potter's own chest and into his lungs the wind went, and there it curled like a worm, and there it stayed. When the worm moved, cold and down so deep, Potter coughed. The Unstoppable Cough. He would try to reach to the bottom of his lungs so that he could scrape that worm out. He would bark like a hound. But the worm was too deep. And then the cough would go on by itself, even when Potter didn't want to cough anymore. On and on, barking and bursting in his throat till all of his air was gone and his lungs had folded flat, but the cough went on anyway, silently, doubling him at the gut, shaking him and making his face swell up. That's why he called it the Unstoppable Cough.

That's why he was in his bedroom, second storey, at the back of the house. His mother said that spring was as bad as winter, because you didn't know what the weather was going to do from one hour to the next, and he should have no fever at all for a week before he went outside. That's why Potter wasn't with Jonathan two days ago when he took his old red hair and went down the hill, laughing like the bang of an ash can, 'Hah, Potter! Ho, Potter! Sixty-dollars-a-day, Potter!'

That's why he was pressing his forehead against the glass.

I could find you, Jonathan!

'No, Potter, absolutely not,' his father had said.

And Potter had asked, 'Why not?'

And his father had frowned as if he were in pain and

whispered, 'We don't want to lose you, too.'

And that had scared Potter so much that he made his own face to go blank, as if he were saying, 'So what? So what?'

But he was really afraid. And what was he afraid of? The river. So what was he staring at now while the evening darkened the hill, the woods, and the ravine? He couldn't see the people combing the ground below the trees. He couldn't see his father or Jonathan's father or Mr Larson. So what was he staring at? Well, the river.

The Red River ran north. The only river to run north. In spring it swelled and grew furious and flooded, because it tried to get into Canada, but it ran against its own old winter ice, and was turned back, enraged. In spring the Red River split its sides, and this was a terrible thing. Into the woods it went, grabbing junk and timber, scouring the trees at their roots, and making a mud on which it was impossible to stand. Angry river. The northflowing river, shut from its destination by its own cold self. Potter was watching the river and remembering what his father had said.

But Potter himself said, 'Come out, come out. O Jonathan, come home again.'

All at once a bird flew up and fluttered against the window, right at Potter's face. He screamed and jumped backward. For a moment the bird breasted the glass, as though trying to find a perch there. It was a redwinged black bird. Then it flew back into the night.

Potter's whole body tingled, and his voice was gone, so that he couldn't answer when his mother called, 'Potter? Potter? Are you all right?'

Just before noon on the following day, everyone stopped looking for Jonathan. They went home. Potter's father, too, came trudging up the hill until he stood on the level grass of the backyard. Potter saw him pause and glance up to the bedroom window. One glance. As soon as he noticed the face of Potter in the window, the man dropped his eyes, stiffened his back, and entered the house; and the screen door banged under Potter's knees.

Then the woods were empty altogether, though the river still chewed at the trees. It was a heavy sky, belly-down and smoky. It might rain later, but you never knew what the weather would do from one hour to the next. That's what his mother said.

Potter's father came into the bedroom. Potter turned and sat on his heels, but his father only looked at him for some time from frowning eyes, and making a hard pinch of his lips.

'Well,' said Potter, 'did everyone go to lunch, then?'

'I suppose so,' said his father.

'Well, are we going to eat soon?'

'Mother will get you something,' said his father.

'Aren't you going to eat?'

'No.'

Potter lowered his voice. 'Is it raining?' he asked.

'No,' said his father.

'So,' said Potter. He put his hands between his knees as if they were cold. He spoke so softly. 'So, if you're not going to eat, and if it isn't raining, then why did you come in so soon?'

Potter's father had very strong forearms. When he folded his arms across his chest, the muscles stood out—and generally he folded his arms when he had nothing to say. Now Potter saw more clearly than ever these silent muscles, the power of his father, and he wished that all the power of his father would go around him in a hug. But he didn't ask for a hug, and his father didn't offer any. Too bad, too bad. Potter was beginning to think that he needed a hug.

His father said, 'I came in to look at my son.'

'Oh,' said Potter. His lip trembled. 'And then will you go out to look for Jonathan again?'

A bird began to flutter at Potter's window, thumping it. Up and down it went, up and down, and its beak made a ticking sound on the glass.

Potter's father looked at the bird instead of at Potter. 'An Oriole wants in,' he said.

'But will you go out to look for Jonathan again?' Potter said.

'Baltimore Oriole,' said his father. And then, still without looking at Potter, he said, 'No. Not again.'

'Why?' said Potter. Somebody should say something straight out. Potter's lip was trembling. 'Why?' But his father was better at folding his arms than at talking.

'No need,' the man said, turning away. 'No reason to.'

It was when the bedroom door was shut that Potter began to cry. Not out loud. Simply, tears spilled and ran down his cheeks.

The Oriole was still fluttering at the window. Potter heard it and turned. An orange and burning bird.

'Go away,' said Potter.

But at exactly that moment the bird began to sing in a clear, sliding whistle, as though calling to Potter through the glass.

'Go away! Go away!' cried Potter, hitting the sill with his fists.

The Oriole flew backward some feet, but then it returned with a stronger will and pecked and scratched the harder.

So Potter threw open the window and waved his arms. 'Do you think I care?' he screamed. 'Ha! I don't want to look at you! Ha! I don't want to hear you, old Baltimore Oriole. Just go away!'

The bird circled and flew to the elm which stood at the side of the yard, half again as high as the house. It was a lovely bird, both black and gold. But Potter slammed the window as though he hated it.

'Do you think I care?' he cried, shaking his finger at the Baltimore Oriole. 'Do you think I care?' he whispered. This was a sentence that Potter suddenly wanted to say again and again.

His mother called him for lunch, and he hollered at the top of his lungs, 'Do you think I care?' He sat down in the centre of the bedroom floor. He folded his arms across his chest. He would holler it again, because when he was hollering he was not crying. He would holler it down the vent to his father in the kitchen below: 'Do—'

But he did not holler it again. He heard his mother's voice instead, and he went very still, listening. He heard his father's voice answering, and he started to sob.

His mother said, 'Ach, Martin, drowned? Drowned, just as you thought, poor boy?'

'Drowned,' said his father. 'But the body lingered on the riverbed, is why we couldn't find him.'

'Oh!' his mother gasped. 'But how—'

'Twig ran through his nose. It held him fast—'

Potter leaped up at that news. Potter spun round three times in the bedroom, as though he were lost, his hands at his ears. Then he drove through the door and down the hall to the top of the stairs.

'Potter, don't you come down here!' said his father at the bottom.

But Potter began to descend, his right hand on the banister.

'Jonathan!' cried Potter. 'Jonathan, what did you do?' he cried, breathing harder and harder. Three steps from the bottom, he threw back his head and wailed, 'I want to see my friend Jona—'

But then the worm twisted in his lungs, and Potter could talk no more. He began to cough great whooping barks, to cough and to cough till all of the air was out of him, and still the worm kept turning, and he coughed no air at all, hanging by one hand from the banister, his face two inches from the floor. But just before he fainted, the strong arms of his father slid under him and caught him, so he did not hit the hard wood.

Oh, Jonathan, Jonathan, who caught you?

The sky kept its promise, that day. Near evening the spring storms broke over the river and ripped the tops of the trees and slammed against Potter's house. It was wild weather from dusk and all through the night. But Potter was not in his bed. Neither was he in the house at all. He was in the back, under three trees.

After supper Potter's parents had left him alone. His mother woke him to see if he wanted to eat. He said, 'Do you think I care?'

She said, 'We're going to Jonathan's house for a while.'

Potter didn't say anything to that, but lay abed with a terrible frown on his face. He folded his arms across his chest. His mother kissed his cheek and left. Potter didn't move. He didn't want to cry any more, and moving might make him cry. He wanted to be angry. The trouble was, there was no one to be angry at. Not at his mother or his father, because it wasn't their fault. Not at Jonathan—he shouldn't be angry at Jonathan. He loved Jonathan. Jonathan was dead. That left two others. He could very easily be angry at God; but Potter was afraid of that, especially now. Or maybe Potter could be angry with Potter?

All at once there came a picking and a pecking at his window, and all at once Potter knew who he was angry at.

Potter sat up in bed and screamed at the top of his lungs, 'Go away!'

The Baltimore Oriole was going up and down the window with its orange belly, the black beak pecking. Busy bird! Old busybody of a bird! It kept trying to come in.

Potter got up, waving his arms. He stomped his foot. 'Do you think I care?' he screamed. It almost felt good to be so angry. 'Go away, you Baltimore Oriole! Get away from me!'

But the bird was very wilful. It never minded the commands of Potter; it kept flying bump against his window.

So Potter ran to the window and threw it open. The bird and the boy went backward from each other just an instant, one flying, one running. But then the bird perched directly on the windowsill, and Potter hated this with all his might. He picked up his baseball.

He cried out, 'Don't you listen to me?' And he threw the baseball at the Oriole. And he hit it. And the bird fell down.

Potter went still, staring where the bird had been. He whispered, 'Oh, no.' Maybe he would cry for sure, now. There was no anger left in Potter, no anger at all. 'Oh, no, no.'

But it was right then that the first winds of the storm began to blow, whipping the backs of the trees and rushing Potter's bedroom, too. Enormous raindrops, eight or twelve of them, bombed the windowpanes, and Potter's heart was turned inside of him.

Potter put his head out of the window. He searched the ground for the Oriole. 'Don't die,' he said. 'I didn't mean it.' And then he called against the wind, 'O Baltimore Oriole, where are you?'

Poor Potter's lip was trembling. He had such pain in his chest for the thing he had done, and he was alone besides! And this was a dangerous storm. So down the stairs went Potter, through the kitchen, out the back door; and down again went Potter to his hands and his knees; under the bushes he went, and his pyjama shirt blew up to his neck.

'Where are you, Baltimore Oriole?'

There it was, lying on its side. Its eye was closed.

Potter picked it up, making a crib of his two hands, and kissed it. 'But I love you,' he said. 'O Baltimore Oriole, what did I do? Don't die. Don't go away like Jonathan went away. I'm so sorry,' said the boy, 'and I love you.'

How thin was the bird's neck, no thicker than matchsticks! Why did God make their necks so thin? Didn't he know how easily they could die? Potter felt the feathers on his upper lip, so soft at the breast of the bird—and then his nose was tweaked.

He stopped kissing the bird.

'Did you do that to me, Baltimore Oriole?' he said holding his breath. Its black eye was open. They looked at each other a moment, and then the bird reached out its beak and distinctly, for the second time, tweaked the nose of Potter.

'Oh, dear Baltimore Oriole,' whispered Potter, 'you are alive. I am so glad.' He gazed at the bird.

But now this boy, crouching underneath the bushes at the back of his house, did a strange thing. Although he was relieved to be twice kissed by the bird, he began to cry. Potter couldn't stop his tears any more, but sobbed and sobbed and held the bird so carefully. Like a little wolf he opened his mouth and wailed to the winds.

And what he said was, 'Baltimore Oriole, I am so lonely.' He said, 'Why do the good friends die? Why couldn't I be dead instead of Jonathan? Oh, oh, I am so lonely!'

The bird moved in his hands. It stood up on the wrist of Potter and cocked its head left and right as though it were watching a curious sight, a boy with his mouth wide open. It was a beautiful bird.

So Potter wept, 'It's no good, dear Baltimore Oriole. How could you be my friend if you can't talk and I can't understand you? Birds can't be Jonathans. I hate Adam. If Adam didn't sin then we could be friends. But this is the way that it is. Birds,' sobbed Potter, 'birds can't know my feelings. You don't know how sad this world is—'

But then the most wonderful thing happened. Potter looked and saw in the Oriole's eye a tear, a single tear of perfect sadness as the bird gazed back at the boy.

Potter whispered, 'You too?'

Suddenly lightning split the heavens apart, arcing from Minnesota to North Dakota, and thunder punched the lungs of Potter. Like nerves aflame the lightning scorched the sky. The wind got up in a furious roar, and now the rain soaked the earth for sure.

'You too?' The boy was filled with gratitude. 'Do you see why I love you so much?' he shouted. 'And I'll protect you, Baltimore Oriole!'

Potter covered the Oriole in his pyjama shirt, and squinted through this wild weather, and ran to the woods. He found a hollow among the roots of three trees, where the wind was weaker and the raindrops dripped but did not sting. He was coughing, now—what he called his Unstoppable Cough. No matter to that: he had a friend, someone to watch out for, and this was the place where he and Jonathan used to hide, a good place. Like a bear cub he curled himself down, the Oriole between his knees and his chest.

Potter was coughing.

One finger of Potter was stroking the head of the Oriole.

Finally, Potter fell asleep.

Jonathan, will you come and play with me tomorrow?

When his father went out with a high-powered searchlight and found the boy, Potter was still smiling. But he had developed a fever. His hands were folded. And his father didn't understand what Potter had done, because there was no bird there any more.

'Why?' said his father when he picked him up. The strong man sounded angry. 'Potter, Potter, why?'

How many days and nights did Potter lie sick after that? He didn't know, nor did he try to count them. Time was squeezing and stretching in front of him like pictures on a rubber balloon.

Potter was hot. His tongue stuck like clay in his mouth. But then Potter would tremble helplessly, frozen colder than the Red River at its Canadian mouth. He drew his knees to his chest, shuddering. But then Potter would throw his covers aside, strip to his underpants, and lie spread-eagle on the sheets, gulping air.

Potter moaned.

His mother came in and put damp cloths on his forehead.

His father stood in the doorway with his arms folded.

He said, 'Potter, why?'

It sounded to Potter as though his father were roaring, a very angry man. Potter couldn't answer him. He didn't know what the man was asking. He could only moan.

His father said, 'Why did you go out in the rain? What?

Did you want to follow Jonathan?'

Follow Jonathan.

'Hush, Martin!' his mother cried, grabbing the boy. 'You oughtn't say such a thing ever—not ever!' And that was all his father said. He left the room. But his mother rocked Potter, talking the loveliest things and singing lullabies as he had never heard them before.

Potter—Potter only moaned.

For what was real, and what wasn't? When was he awake, and when was he asleep? All the world went sliding in his poor head. He could not tell truly whether his eyes were open and he saw, or whether they were closed and he dreamed. Powerful were the dreams in him during those days.

This was a very sick Potter.

Then he noticed that the singing of his mother had changed. In the deep, invisible darkness it rose to a lightsome whistle: *Dee-dit, dah-der, dee-dit,* over and over again, appealing to the sweet soul of the boy and causing him to weep for the very beauty of the sound. *Dee-dit, dah-der, dee-dit.*

Once, while the wonderful melody filled his ears, he felt a fine breeze across his face, a wind so cool that it blew the fever from his forehead.

Mother, are you fanning me? he asked.

His mother did not answer him; but the song still trembled in the bedroom, and he looked, and he saw above him on the bedstead the Baltimore Oriole. See? The window was open! And see? The bird was straking its two wings through the air making such a gentle breeze and singing this song: 'Dee-dit, dah-der, dee-dit.'

Well, said Potter, reaching up his hand and smiling, *so you came back after all. I knew that you would come back, my friend.*

But before his hand could reach as high as the Oriole, Potter was sleeping again—more peacefully than ever since Jonathan had gone.

But other nights and other darknesses were different from this one.

Potter would get out of bed crying, *Jonathan! Jonathan!* He crawled on the floor looking for his friend. Under the bed? No, not there. What would Jonathan be doing under the bed. Behind the door? In the closet? No, no. Outside? Outside! Waiting to play!

Jonathan! Potter called as he crawled to the window, aching with loneliness. *Jonathan, where are you now?*

But Potter's mother would come saying, 'Hush, Potter. O my Potter, hush.' And she would hold him to her breast, and Potter would say, *Red hair is too real to die.* She would shake her head and say, 'God wanted Jonathan to come be home with him in heaven. Hush, Potter. You'll only break your heart to think on things that cannot be.'

If God took Jonathan away from me, said Potter, *then I hate God.* But maybe his mother didn't hear what he said, because she went on rocking him and saying, 'God came and took your friend—'

Then Potter looked over his mother's shoulder and saw the Baltimore Oriole perched outside the window. And behold, the bird understood! The Oriole was weeping just as Potter himself was weeping. No words. No talk of God. No song. But open eyes and tears.

O my friend! cried Potter. *I'm so glad to see you!*

Potter stretched out his arms and tried to get up. He struggled against his mother. She could barely restrain him, for the desire to hold the Oriole again was very strong in him.

'Martin!' screamed his mother. 'Martin, help me!'

So his father came and took the boy by his shoulders. His father was too, too strong. Immediately his mother shut the window.

Mama! Potter wailed like a wolf cub. *Mama, don't!*

She knelt beside him. She was crying, too. 'My poor, poor Potter,' she said, 'please hush and let it all come right.'

But Potter pulled his knees up to his chest and pretended to be sleeping. When his parents left the room, the child arose with terrible pain and dizziness and went to the window and gritted his teeth and opened it a crack. Then he fell upon the bed again.

He was only a boy. Nevertheless, with the weight of a great elm tree he toppled down in tiredness.

'Eat it, Potter, eat it.'

Potter popped open his eyes. Night-time. He was wide awake and lost. He thought that he had been coughing, but he wasn't coughing now, and things were cold and clear around him. The boy held still, lest he fall off something. He turned his eyes left and right, and there was the dresser, his dresser, three drawers closed and one stuck out like a tongue; and there was his desk and the lamp lit dim and his books and pencils; and, yes, that was the place he used to sit reading *Jerry Todd* and Hans Andersen and Ovid; and here were his own covers kicked low, and there was the window still open its crack: Potter's room. This was Potter's bedroom—not so strange after all. But it had never been so sharp to his seeing before, as though he were Potter in a flash photograph.

'Eat it, Potter, eat it.'

He lay naked, except for his underpants. The sky was deep green outside his window, the horizon black. The river would be the deepest thing in that horizon, like a slash, a cut in the earth, like a snake belly-down forever north, forever south and silent and sliding and terrible, and Potter hated it.

Suddenly something dropped to the sheet beside him. Now he turned his head, and there was the Baltimore Oriole, not two feet from his face. Potter smiled immediately. The Oriole bowed and said, 'Dee-dit, dah-der, dee-dit,' nodding and bowing low.

Oh, hello, Baltimore Oriole, said Potter. He moved his hand to touch the bird, but it hopped just out of reach and he was a very slow boy in his sickness.

The bird spoke again, still nodding; but this time Potter's eyes widened and his mouth dropped open. The bird said, 'Dee-dit, Potter, eat it. Eat it, Potter, eat it.'

Poor Potter. The heart in the boy began to beat with dangerous violence, and his temples ached. *Oh, no!* he cried. *What are you doing? Did you hear what you just said, Baltimore Oriole?* The boy put his hands to his cheeks. *You said my name! Oh, no! And besides that, I understood you. O dear Baltimore Oriole, what are we doing? We're talking!*

Poor Potter. He felt that he was going to cry again, this time for fear.

The best things in the world are treasures. But treasures might be lost or stolen. Didn't Potter know as much on account of Jonathan? And here was the most splendid treasure of all, hardly to be believed, that he and the bird might be friends, talking, talking, passing the time of day. So if this were really true, how terrifying to think that he could lose this, too!

But the Oriole was not dismayed. The Oriole had business to do, and do it the beautiful bird did. It fluttered to the toe of Potter and perched there. This tickled the boy. Next it flew to his chest and put its black eye, by a half cock, directly in front of Potter's face. 'Eat it, Potter, eat it,' it said, nodding with the sternest authority. Then it jumped to the sheet and picked in one claw three silken leaves and held them up and repeated the command, 'Eat it, Potter, eat it.'

Potter held his breath, watching. Potter didn't budge a muscle.

So the Oriole laid one leaf on his left hand and one leaf on his right and one leaf—while poor Potter crossed his eyes—lightly on his lips.

'Mugwort, Potter,' the bird announced, proud of itself. 'Eat muggins in May. You eat it, Potter. Eat it.'

Slowly, Potter put out his tongue. The leaf stuck to it like a feather. All at once the Oriole touched its head beneath a wing and made a tiny sound like sneezing: *ker-poop!*

But that was no sneeze, and Potter knew it. Even to a bird, a cross-eyed boy with his tongue stuck out looked silly. The Baltimore Oriole was laughing.

'Pretty Potter! Pretty Potter! *Ker-poop!*'

Potter, in spite of himself, said, *Hee-hee!* Next, he giggled, and from giggling he went to chuckling. So then they were friends together, laughing together—and that made all the difference. Right easily the boy began to chew the mugwort, and the one in his left hand, and the one in his right, all three, a cheerful little snack.

But then the game that had begun funny turned very, very serious.

Bitter were the mugwort leaves. Spit flooded Potter's mouth, and his eyes ran tears, and he swallowed. Then his nostrils flared, the better to breathe, and his whole body went to tingling, and a great lump formed in his stomach where the bitter oils had run.

Nobody was laughing now.

Baltimore Oriole, Potter gasped, *what is happening to me?*

From far away and solemnly the Oriole sang his song, 'Eat it, Potter, eat it.'

Potter's stomach tightened and his mouth opened up, as though to vomit. His skinny muscles contracted around the lump, pushing it forward, and he thought that he would suffocate when it came thick into his throat.

Ba, Ba, Baltimore! he cried, frightened. He was such a small boy.

Potter's mouth yawned as wide as a cave, and his throat went vastly hollow, and the lump squeezed higher and higher, and then he threw back his head. He arched his spine in a spasm. But he could not scream any more, because the lump was coming.

He heard the Oriole calling, 'Push, Potter, push!'

Potter pushed. He wanted to breathe. He was dying, the huge lump jammed at the back of his tongue—

Then suddenly came the most amazing change. All at once Potter was *in* a cave, rising from the deepest reaches of the earth. He was being pushed out of a damp, dark hole to air and to freedom. With strong scratchings of his feet he climbed, and he cried, *Wait for me! Wait for me!*

Potter wasn't dying at all. He was being born.

At the mouth of the cave hung stalactites like teeth, and like teeth the stalagmites stood up. Potter crawled between them. His head felt a cool breeze, and how grateful he was to breathe again! Then his shoulders and his back and his stomach squeezed out—and he was free.

And behold! Here was the Baltimore Oriole beside him, a definite twinkle in both its eyes and warm words singing: 'Welcome, Potter, welcome.' But the bird was now exactly the size of Potter himself! They were the same.

But everything else was different. His bedroom had grown enormous, his dresser as big as a four-storey house, his desk was a mesa, his bed was a wilderness.

Potter said to the Oriole, *Friends?* He figured he needed a friend to trust in if the world was going to swell and surprise him.

And then it was a blessing that the Oriole answered, 'Friends, dear Potter,' because the next sight was a shock.

There, on his back in the centre of the bed, lay a little boy, naked except for his underpants, his eyes rolled up, his mouth wide open.

That's me! Potter cried, running backward. *That's Potter there!*

How skinny was that body, how pale and helpless. Potter wanted to cry for what he saw.

But the Oriole came and kissed his neck. 'Shhh, Potter,' said the Oriole. 'This is you here, somebody that I'm kissing. This is the soul of you, set free. And I set you free for a reason, a very good reason. Oh, Potter, come ride the wind with me.'

I came out of my mouth, said Potter, still staring at the little boy.

'Aye,' said the Oriole orange. 'To soar the sky with me.'

I—I left my self behind.

'Aye. To learn the holy things of God, because you asked me.'

Baltimore Oriole, Potter whispered as though they were in church, *am I dead?*

'Nay, Potter,' laughed the Oriole gentle. 'Nay, and never more alive. Oh, Potter, look at yourself. You are a bird, now.'

Indeed. He was a bird. A dumpy sort of bird, to be sure, a little head on a lumpish body, doughy at the breast of him, his wings crossed at his lower back, and a song, when he sang, so mournful as to break your heart—but a bird nevertheless.

'A dove,' said the Oriole. 'Oh, come on, Potter, Dove-Potter. Come fly with me!'

Straightway the Oriole twitted to the window and was gone.

Well, that left a lonely bedroom and the smell of sickness,

and Potter did not want to stay there. So he followed. He waddled across the bedroom floor, thrusting his head forward like a chicken. He jumped to the windowsill, and without a second thought he slipped into the night.

Ooooooooooooriole! screamed Potter. He was falling like an open sheet.

'Wings, Potter!' cried the Oriole. 'Open your wings!'

He did. And what happened then was a wonder of the mighty God and a gift to Potter forever.

When just above the bushes his wings went out, they caught the air like sheaves of wheat beneath his shoulders, and suddenly he was sailing level to the ground at an easy speed.

Potter began to laugh. He tightened a muscle above his butt; his tail fanned forward, and he soared up. Mighty flaps of his wings—clumsy flaps, since the wing tips slapped above and below his body—powerful flaps, and he arose. He lunged higher and higher. Up the side of the house; up so high he cleared the elm; up and up and loose and free until the city lights turned below him, the river a ribbon of darkness, the woods like fur on the back of a bear.

Potter gulped the glory of God, the goodness of creation, and all of heaven stretched around him. He laughed like a loon, a little crazy to have let go of the earth, to float at the tops of the clouds.

Ha, ha! Swoop to the left, Dove-Potter, why not? He did. And swoop to the right, you light-hearted bird. He did. Then dive, child, dive like a hawk straight down from the clouds, your feathers thrumming at such high speeds, your eyes made narrow by streaking the winds. He did. He did: like an arrow piercing down to the earth and whistling the wind, he did!

Suddenly: 'Potter!'

The name came from behind his head. He stumbled in the air, tumbled, and hit the ground. He bounced. Oh, awkward, to be on one's feet again.

'Potter,' said the Oriole, 'this has been good, and I laughed when you laughed, and your gladness has made me glad. But you have to go back to you again.'

This is so wonderful, Baltimore Oriole, said Potter, full of chatter. *I never knew that I could be so light. Why don't we tell all the children—*

'Potter! Your mother is soon to look in on you—'

And what will I do? I'll tell her about flying.

'Please, Potter, you don't understand. When she sees the body-you, she will think that you are dead.'

Dead? Coldness shot through Potter's body, and the night was dark after all, and his little window at the second floor glowed orange. *Dead?* Oh, the sad earth!

'And she will cry,' said the Oriole.

Mama! My mama!

'Up, now, Potter. Come up for the love of your mother.'

Quickly, then, they flew to the ledge of his bedroom window, and they entered in. Potter looked at himself, the sickly boy with his mouth wide open and his back twisted. Potter felt sorry for him. But then he saw himself in the way that his mother might see him: thin legs, thin arms, no motion in her son, no greeting in his eyes, and he hurt for her. What would his mother say, if she saw no life in Potter?

Therefore, Potter-the-bird went up to the mouth of Potter-the-boy and prepared to climb down the cave again. Down the damp hole, down the dark he would go, on account of his mother, down to the bottom of clay and buried—

Suddenly Potter was afraid. He turned to the Oriole, still perched on the windowsill.

Friends? he pleaded.

'Friends,' said the Oriole.

I won't lose you, please, the way that I lost Jonathan?

'Oh, Potter, this is just the beginning,' said the Oriole. 'There is a reason why I brought you out of yourself. I will show you what's become of Jonathan—'

He drowned, said Potter.

'Hush. Hush that, Potter,' said the Oriole. 'And this is the reason: because you held me, child of Adam, and because you loved me.'

So Potter remembered the promise. He put his head into his mouth and struggled down his throat with trouble. There came the moment when he thought he could not breathe: the bird was smothered and the boy was choking. But that moment passed when he broke into a long, long cough, and his boy's body rolled over on the bed, wracked with his terrible coughing.

His mother came in and took his head between her hands. Potter wept to feel the coolness of her hands. He grabbed them and held on with all his might.

'My poor, poor baby,' she said.

Oh, Mama, Mama.

The coughing ended, finally, leaving Potter all exhausted

and covered with sweat. But he smiled a little smile at her, for he loved her and he loved touching her, and there was a part of him that had never been so happy.

'I think you had a nightmare, Potter,' she said.

But the Oriole sang in the morning dusk, 'Dee-dit, dah-der, dee-dit.'

In the days when Potter was a boy and sick, the doctors did not have penicillins for healing, no shots to shoot the fever down. Therefore, children had to fight fevers with the strength of their own small bodies, and often no one knew who'd be the stronger, the boy or the fever. If the boy, then the fever went away. But if the fever, then they both departed to the everlasting cold, zero at the bone.

A boy could die.

And there was a name for the worst period of the disease. When the boy and the fever fought each other the hardest— when they wrestled desperately to death or to health again— that was called the 'crisis'. Parents agonized during the 'crisis'. They couldn't sleep. They sat by their child, praying, wiping his forehead in cool cloths, wishing that they could fight the fiery enemy for him and sad that they could not. Parents paced in their kitchens under yellow light bulbs, deep at night. They drank coffee. Sometimes they just stared at one another, as though someone might say something magical and their child would come downstairs yawning and asking for a drink of water. But no. They wouldn't say anything at all. There was nothing magical to say. What they did during the 'crisis' was, they waited.

The 'crisis' might last for three hours before the child sighed and slipped into a deeper sleep of one sort or another: three hours, seven hours, thirteen hours.

Potter's 'crisis' lasted three days. Ah, Potter! He was such a skinny child.

It began the evening after his mother had said, 'You had a nightmare.' She was closing the curtains in his room and she was just about to shut the window, too, when Potter said right clearly, 'It's too tight.'

'What, baby?' said his mother, smiling, one hand on the sash.

'It's too tight,' said Potter.

And this is why his mother was smiling: Potter had no covers on. No pyjamas. Nothing was tight on him. He was acting silly, and that made his mother glad. 'Go to sleep, rapscallion,' she said.

But the boy suddenly burst into the most desolated howl. Oh, the lonely wolf cub! No one understood his sorrow. 'It's too tight! It's too tight! Mama, it's too *tight*!' wailed Potter.

'What, baby? What's too tight?' His mother wasn't smiling, now, but perplexed. She stepped toward his bed. His eyes were closed. 'Are you sleeping,' she whispered, 'and dreaming after all?'

Potter said, 'My body.' He turned and howled, 'My *body* is too tight on me!'

She didn't understand this saying, but neither did she try to. For when she came to Potter's bed, and when she touched his forehead, she was terrified.

'Martin!' she shrieked. She had never screamed like that before. She had never been so scared. 'Martin! Martin! Potter's burning up!' Then she mumbled, 'Potter, oh, Potter, Potter, Potter,' feeling his cheeks with her own cheek, sliding her hands all down his body. 'MARTIN! HURRY!'

Paper dry was Potter's skin. His face, forehead, and throat were red as flame. The bridge of his nose was white. He was breathing breaths no deeper than a sparrow's, tiny, tiny puffs of nothing.

'My body is. Too tight for. Me.'

'He's delirious,' Potter's mother chattered when his father strode in. 'I think that he is one hundred and six degrees. Oh, Martin! A fever this high could ruin his brain. You know, you know. A fever like this could stop his—Oh, Martin!'

Potter's father said nothing at all. But, smelling of wood, his strong arms covered with sawdust, he lifted his son into the air and bore him from the room.

Potter remembered forever the smell of wood as the smell of the nearness of God; and the feel of sawdust on his cheek was the stuff of love. Whenever thereafter the saws would cut to the heart of the white pine, Potter would fall silent and whisper in his soul, 'Ah, this is sacred.'

So down the stairs went Potter in the cradle of his father's arms, thin legs swinging. In the kitchen the man gathered the whole boy under one arm. With the other he dragged a steel tub from under the sink. He attached a hose to the tap, then shot water into the tub—all in a few seconds. He was very stern. He was very strong.

The water foamed and swirled beneath its steady jet.

Potter's father breathed through his nose, which whistled.

Potter's mother said, 'I'm going to Larsons. I'll ask them to get the doctor. They'll do that. I'll be back.'

His mother could not stand still.

The steel tub swelled with water. Potter's father went down on his knees beside it, his son straight out in front of him, held almost like a tender prayer, or sacrifice. And then the man let the boy by inches sink into the water.

It was so cold! Potter thrashed with his arms and sucked air. He hit his father hard on the lip, and the lip began to bleed, but his father did not move a whit and the boy didn't know what he had done. He was just shocked by the freezing water. His scalp and neck and skin all shrivelled on his body.

And while he was in the water, he woke up. He looked and he saw his father's face all covered with sawdust and pain, and this was a new thing for the boy, a most curious thing, for he had never seen his father in pain before, never before in pain.

'Are you all right, Poppi?' he asked.

His father nodded.

'Did you know that you are bleeding?'

His father shook his head, but he did nothing to wipe the red run of blood from his chin, because both his arms were under Potter.

So Potter stuck out his pointer finger and dabbed the blood away, and sawdust and whisker-grit were in that dab. And when he felt the stiffness of his father's whiskers, Potter said, 'I love you, Poppi.'

Immediately the mouth of Potter's father drew tight, and white went his face, and hard his eyes, and frowning his brow. Potter's father neither looked at him nor said a word, but that was okay with Potter. Potter was used to his father by now.

Then Potter sighed and seemed to fall asleep, resting his head on his father's shoulder.

In a little while his mother came back. Right behind her Mrs Larson bustled in with the biggest bottom in all the world and great arms that could never hang straight down because, like the sides of pyramids, they had to make room for Mrs Larson's bottom, seventeen feet from one side to the other. Mrs Larson had enormous quantities of sympathy, had gallons of pity, whole oceans of compassion—and she kept it all inside her bottom. That's what Jonathan said.

When Mrs Larson wanted to help the weak, the heavy laden, cumbered with a load of care, no man could stop her, and it didn't matter the time, night or midnight. Look out for Mrs Larson, when she came to heal you! And how did she heal you? She cooked. She baked. She boiled and fried and diced. She measured and whipped and covered the kitchen in flour and generally caused food to happen everywhere.

This she began to do the instant that she saw Potter in his tub, so the kitchen was full of Mrs Larson.

Soon the doctor came as well, and after him came Mr Larson with a raw, red face, and then who could move in such a crowd? Who could breathe? The doctor examined Potter. 'Yep. The "crisis",' he said. 'You'll have to watch him, now. Keep water in your tub. If he can swallow, give him liquids. Liquids—that's the order of the day. Fluids till his nostrils dribble—'

Mrs Larson switched at once from cakes to broth.

Mr Larson looked superficial. He didn't know where to put his hands. He didn't know where to put himself. He always followed Mrs Larson.

Potter's mother felt duty-bound to care for all these people. But Potter's father did not.

When the boy was cool, it didn't matter who was talking, who was cooking, or who was drinking coffee. The man rose up with his son raining water all over the floor, and he left the kitchen. He wrapped the boy in a towel and carried him to his bedroom and dried him with vigorous rubbings all over his body, and Potter opened his eyes again.

Potter smiled. He liked this touch of his father.

Potter's father saw that and began to clear his throat with much violence, and then he did an extraordinary thing.

He said, 'Can you hear me?'

Potter said, 'Yes, Poppi.'

'And do you remember what you said downstairs?' he asked.

Potter said, 'Yes, Poppi.'

'Well,' said his father, blinking rapidly, 'I feel the same way, too, Potter.'

Immediately the man stood straight up and folded his arms across his chest and put a fierce look on his face. And Potter laughed.

Oh, Potter knew what it cost his father to say such a thing. Potter knew the wonder that had just taken place, for Potter had never, never heard his father to hint at love before. How dearly he wanted to pay his father back for such a kindness.

But what did he have to give him? Ah, Poppi! Then Potter grinned, for he thought that he would tell his father his secret, this for his father alone.

'I can fly,' he said.

Potter's father nodded.

'This is true,' said Potter. 'I can fly. I flied yesterday sometime. I went out that window, and I was very happy. Poppi, I wasn't sick at all. The Unstoppable Cough was gone.'

Potter noticed the bit of a smile at his father's lips and kind eyes crinkling down on him. This made Potter's heart to rejoice, because he was giving his father some happiness, too. So he chattered on, telling more and more.

'Do you remember the Baltimore Oriole at my window, yes? Well, he comes back, you see. He is my friend. He comes in the crack there. He talks with me in English, and I am a dove, and we go out the window together—'

The man's smile faded. He glanced at the window, a gathering frown on his forehead. But Potter's tongue was loose, and he went on.

'You think the tree is high? Ho, I flied a hundred times higher than that. And this is just the beginning, Poppi. I'm going out the window again, because the Oriole promised it to me, and we are going to follow Jonathan, to find out where he went. I'm going to find my dear friend Jonathan— Poppi? Poppi? *Oh, Father, no!*' cried the boy.

For his father had left him. The man had suddenly turned from his son and had gone to the window and had shut it with an absolute bang. Then he turned round to Potter with a very angry face.

'Jonathan is dead,' he said.

'I know,' said Potter.

'Drowned,' said the man. Potter's eyes began to sting with tears.

'I know,' he said.

'But not you! Not you, Potter!'

Potter said, 'Why are you so angry?'

'You, Potter, are not going to die. Do you hear me?'

In his mind the boy said, *I hear you.* But all he could do out loud was to cry, for both the sadness and the fever were catching him away again, stealing Potter, the one like an eagle, the other a rook.

'Potter!' The nostrils of his father were flaring. Oh, why was he so angry? 'Potter, you are my son.' His eyes were red, were wet. 'You will forget this following of Jonathan—'

Open the window, Father, Potter said. *Please, Poppi, open the window so that the Baltimore Oriole could come in again. Please.*

But his father did not so much as look at the window under his great thunderclap of a frown. He was squeezing his eyes shut. He left the room.

Potter was alone.

Then the fever attacked him again, and they began to wrestle. Life and death. Life or death. Potter had entered his 'crisis'.

Potter began to pray. He got the idea from his mother. This poor lady prayed endless prayers around Potter these days, stroking and stroking his hair.

She prayed: 'Mighty God, O let me have my child some

little longer, yet. Don't take him from me. I will be so empty if you take my boy away from me. And what could you want with a child who has done nothing yet? Neither greatness nor sinning is in my Potter. He hasn't had the time. So what kind of a God would you be to give and to take so quickly? It would be a terrible mistake. And how, and how—' She trembled with her prayer. 'And how could I love you if you snatched my Potter from my house?'

But Potter prayed: *Let me follow Jonathan. Please let me see what happened to my friend Jonathan. O God, I know why I am sick. Because it isn't finished yet. Not until, not until—*

This was Potter's prayer. But it all came out in a single word. The boy would throw his head to the left and to the right and howl at the top of his lungs: 'Jonathan!'

Deep under the river, wreathed in a flowing riverweed, rolling with the current of cold waters, was a boy. His mouth was open. Little fishes darted through his cloud of ruddy hair. And one crooked twig, like a witch's finger, came out of the mud and caught him at the nostril.

'Jonathaaaaaan!'

It was a horrible sight.

It had to be cancelled, done away with forever, abolished, forgotten, atoned, forgiven, *answered*! Or else Potter could never live in peace again.

'Oh, God! Oh, Jonathaaaaaan!'

Potter woke up with his own voice still circling the air of his bedroom. He was panting like a dog in August, sweat running the whole of his skinny body. His hair was matted to his forehead, and he stank. He was alone.

Two birds fluttered at the window. The Oriole, its beak full of leaves, bumped glass like a tennis ball. Very urgent, it was, and Potter knew that the time had come.

The other bird was black in every respect, except with red at its shoulders. It was as skilful on the wing as the Oriole; but it shied from the glass, from the window and the house. It hadn't the boldness of its companion.

Potter looked at them and shook his head. His mouth was yanked back at the corners, as if grinning. But he wasn't grinning. He was trying not to cry. It seemed to him that his friend was calling, and he could not answer. It seemed to him that the bird was going away forever and with it the joy of Jonathan. It seemed to him that holiness was on the other side of the window, and the window was locked.

Potter hid his face in the pillow.

Go away, he said.

Then he heard the dear song of the bird: 'Eat it, Potter, eat it,' and that made his soul to ache for loneliness.

Oh! Oh, please, wept Potter, *I cannot go!*

But an insistent drumming was set up at the window. The Oriole pecked like seconds on a clock, as light as cottonwood. And with such loving the Oriole called, 'Here, dear! Come right here!'

So Potter, still holding the pillow in front of his face, got up from bed. A swooning swept over him, and he veered to the left, and he would have fainted, except that the pecking called him, the pecking focused him, and he stumbled blindly to the pecking. He gasped. He bowed his head and toppled forward. Pillow and head, he hit the window, which shattered raining glass adown the bushes. And Potter slumped to the floor.

Straightway the Oriole was at his side, and the leaves were pressed against his lips. As though he were an infant with his mouth agape, he let the Oriole feed him, for he had no strength to help. He chewed the bitter leaves. He swallowed the bitter oils, and the lump arose in his gut again, and the spasms grabbed and pushed it forward. How pitifully his skinny stomach squeezed the lump! How weakly it climbed to his throat. But it came.

And soon Potter, the soul of Potter, lightsome, bright and glorious, sprang free of his own stiff self. He shook his feathers like metal foil.

Here I am, said Potter the dove. He was breathless, laughing.

'All in good time, good Potter,' said the Oriole, more beautiful than ever before, golden, black, and shining. 'All in good time.'

Friends? said Potter.

'Friends,' said the Oriole. 'Quickly, let's go.'

And by double swoops above the body of a boy, by flight through a broken window they went.

'Potter, you shouldn't hate your body.'

This is what the Baltimore Oriole said when they had flown some time at the top of the sky, streaking beneath the firmament. Potter flew beside it, mystified by the endless, easy beating of his own wings and by the roundness of the earth below and by the silence. But this was no lonely silence, for the thoughts of the stars were everywhere here, and they thought in melody.

East, east and south the bird and Potter flew, a half a continent in darkness when heaven was bright and peopled but America was black: two friends too high for anyone to know their passage, two birds free. Then the morning rushed toward them and they were above the ocean, its waters first golden in the dawning, then brassy by the sunlight, and then aluminium at noon. Sometimes clouds, like angels' breath, blew backward underneath their bellies, so that Potter wondered at his speed; but never did he tire. Nor ever did he cease to exalt in the winds that lifted him.

Baltimore Oriole, I do not hate my body, he called. *I feel sorry for it. It can't fly.*

'Oh, it can fly higher than I,' cried the Oriole, 'by thinking alone. Just by thinking. It can think the galaxies, dear Potter my brother; and then, by two swift thoughts, it has gone to travel among them.'

But it coughs, Baltimore Oriole, and it is sick. Poor skinny ribs, poor naked knees still bunched on my bedroom floor! How could anyone like that little dishrag—a boy?

'I do,' called the Oriole. 'I envy the body of a boy.'

You? Beautiful Baltimore Oriole, I cry to see your freedom and to hear your song. Why should you wish you were me?

'Ah, Potter, Potter! When God came down to live among the creatures of the earth, did he stop in the sky and become a bird? Nay, but he was born of a woman and he became a human being. Pish, but I think there's a dummy in Potter.'

On and on they flew, caught in a headlong wind that took

the miles like a snake's tongue, darting.

'This is the Brave Westerly,' called the Oriole.

Who is? Potter saw no one about.

'The wind whose back we are riding.'

Oh, said Potter. *Hello, Brave Westerly*, he said.

A frowning crag of land crawled toward them through the ocean. To this they descended. On its massive forehead they rested, and the wind went on without them for a while.

Potter said, *What is this place?*

The Oriole answered, 'The end of the earth. A rock, Potter.'

Does he have a name, too?

'Gibraltar.'

Hello, Gibraltar, said Potter. He was happy and excited, and you never knew: anything at all might want to be the friend of a bird—now that Potter was a bird.

High above them, far ahead of them, Potter saw a dot in the sky, and he thought it was the canny blackbird, red at the shoulder, which was a surprise to him, that this fellow would be going in the same direction as they were going. How nice!

Potter turned to the Oriole to ask about this, but the Oriole had already launched itself into the air, crying, 'Up, Potter, up. If you are to see the whole of the story, we've got to get there first, before the night!'

Now they crossed a sea so azure and so clear that the hills and the valleys underwater lay like a map beneath their seeing.

'Five hundred years,' sang the Oriole a misty song: 'Once

with every half one thousand years, the story of God takes place for us, and the birds are reminded, and the birds remember. The birds know the love of God. Hurry, Potter, that you might see the story. Hurry, my brother, that you might know it, too—'

Like a blazing bullet, a tracer, the Oriole sped ahead, and together they shot over land, leaving the sea behind. This was yellow desert, windswept and blistered, blown into the yawning shapes of desolation: lonely land, dry for miles around, a wilderness.

'There!' cried the Oriole, nearly bursting with anticipation. Potter grinned. His friend had never been so giddy before. 'There! There! Do you see him, Potter?'

But the sun behind them was so low that it made streaks of deep purple across the desert, shadows that swallowed the sight. Potter saw nothing.

'Oh, Potter! Dear Potter, look! Just once in a hundred times five! Look! The Phoenix!'

Felix? said Potter, squinting.

He saw an island of greensward in the middle of the wilderness, and in the middle of that a fountain of trees, some of them high, one of them higher than all the others, leaning and hanging its leaves like the hair of a woman. Palm trees.

Suddenly, *Felix!* screamed Potter. *I see him!*

Oh, the magnificent bird that Potter saw, sinking down upon the tallest tree! Potter felt tiny at that size, as great as an eagle's, and the colours of the creature dazzled his eyes: gold at the neck, deep purple for the rest of his body, a tail azure-blue inmixed like a king's robe with feathers of rose, and his head was set with a crest most curiously wrought.

Little Potter and the gladsome Oriole perched in a lesser tree, held very still, and watched.

The Phoenix was building a great nest, the materials of which cast a scent upon the evening air so sweet that Potter moaned. Altogether, he felt a dread to be spying on this splendid presence. He loved him suddenly; but he feared him, too. What if *Felix* should turn an eye and notice Potter? Why, Potter would bow his head and die. See what fine intelligence directed every move the Phoenix made! Nothing was wasted: sticks of cinnamon and—though Potter couldn't name the orient spices frankincense and myrrh and spikenard, these were the bed of the holy bird. And when all was done, he sighed and settled and rested.

Potter burst into tears.

'Why are you crying, Potter?' whispered the Oriole.

I don't know, said Potter. *He is so old, so tired.*

'Five hundred years old,' said the Oriole quietly.

I want to kiss him, said Potter.

'You can't,' said the Oriole. 'He is attending to a greater work right now.'

I know, said Potter. *That's why I'm crying. He is so noble and so lonely, and I wish I were more beautiful—*

Despite their flight, neither of the two friends slept that night, for the air itself trembled with the terrible thing to come. Each time the Phoenix sighed in his nest, Potter's heart jumped.

He said, *Where did Felix come from?*

The Oriole said, 'Out of Paradise, my brother, because there can be no dying in Paradise.'

So far east were Potter and the Oriole that they could see the break of the morning, so close to the early sun that Potter caught his breath and whispered, *Oriole?* The sun was a living being, but one to whom poor Potter couldn't say, *Hello*.

Up the horizon charged the sun, wild and hot and golden. With blasts of the nostril, clattering hooves, he broke the stables, he leaped to the dome of the sky, he ascended, burning, burning. Potter cried, *Oriole?* Some things it is better not to know. What Potter saw, bright in the midst of the fire, was a flaming chariot and four horses each with a shooting eye and the image of a man at the reins. Great were the horses, greater the hands that held them, and terrible the might of the five. But he saw this dimly, as though beaten on a golden dish. *Oriole, was it always this way?*

Potter was frightened.

Then the Phoenix slowly arose on his nest and draped his tail behind. Gravely he watched the coming sun, his colours shimmering. Unmoved he heard the thunder of the hooves. He did not hide. He waited.

When the sun had galloped close above him, the horses straining their necks and the man his shoulders, the Phoenix threw up his head, and the Phoenix began to sing.

Dear God, what a song that was! As though his throat were the pipe of an organ, he made the air to tremble with deep music, woeful majesty at the mouth of the Phoenix and trumpets of supplication. He played pathetic melodies among the baritones, for his memory was long and grievous. Oboes wept and the flutes accused. What did the Phoenix sing? He sang five hundred years of wars. In his song the men went down with bloody strings, and the women hung their heads in elegies, and cannon were the kettledrums between. The Phoenix sang of the sorrow of men, of the fightings and dyings in half one thousand years, and his song was grand, and his song was sad at once.

Stop! screamed Potter, covering his ears. The causes of death were too many for his poor head. *I'm only a boy!*

'A soul,' called the Oriole, 'and a soul can know the truth!'

But the Phoenix did not sing for Potter. The Phoenix was singing for the sun, and the sun indeed did stop. He reined his chargers backward and dipped a golden ear toward earth, for the song enchanted him. And when the sun stopped, and while the horses stood restrained, the whole world stopped as well: the moon, the stars, and the planet earth all paused in their turning round. Even the angels fell silent. It was a tremendous, mournful thing, all at once to hear the suffering of the people gathered into one sole throat, to hear what the mouth of the Phoenix sang.

As long as the Phoenix uttered his music, the universe held absolutely still.

But then the Phoenix himself gave up the song, too terrible to bear, and bowed his head. Silence. In that moment the sun loosed his reins. The horses felt the slack and bounded up with a greater speed. Their hooves struck sparks from the firmament. The sparks rained burning upon the earth, and they caught in the nest of the Phoenix, and the nest burst into flame. The Phoenix did not so much as raise his head; he seemed to know that this would be the result of his song, and maybe it was the purpose. A sweet, blue fire hissed in the spices beneath him. Smoke closed over him. But the Phoenix kept his head bowed down and did not move.

Felix! screamed Potter. *Oh, Felix, fly away!*

The Phoenix did not.

Instead, his own bright feathers caught fire. His tail became a torch and his wings spread out spilling flames, and he laid his head across the coals and allowed himself to be swallowed in the burning.

And he died.

Poor Potter sobbed and sobbed. Again and again he wailed the sorrow of the mourning dove, unable to look at the char and the smoke arising from the tallest palm tree, and all was silence in the wilderness, save his wailing.

'Hush, Potter,' said the Oriole. 'This is the story. This is the way that it is supposed to be.'

But I loved him, Potter wept.

'And he loved you,' said the Oriole.

Oh, Baltimore Oriole, Felix didn't even know me.

'Yes, he did. By name,' said the Oriole.

But Potter was brokenhearted. Potter could not be comforted. Was this what he had come to see, the death of a friend greater than his first friend? Potter decided that there was nothing left in all the world, nothing good nor valuable any more. Death was more real than anything else, so everything else was a lie.

The Oriole said, 'Potter, this is not the end of the story.'

But Potter neither answered nor looked at his friend. He put his dove's head underneath his wing and determined to hide there forever. *Do you think I care?* Tough Potter. Scornful Potter. Potter the pagan, believing in nothing since nothing was honest at all.

Potter pouted.

A whole day Potter stayed that way, hiding.

The Oriole said, 'I brought you to see the story, Potter, and here you are, and isn't it strange that I have to *tell* it to you after all?' Potter didn't answer. So the Oriole said, 'There is a worm in the ashes of the Phoenix. Listen. You can hear it stirring.'

Tsht. Tshhht. Potter heard the little curling. But Potter did not believe.

On the second day of his pout, the Oriole said, 'Oh, Potter, you're missing a miracle. The worm is swelling up. And what was hair, like the hair of a caterpillar, why that is feathers now. This is the story, don't you know.'

Potter, twice bereft, saw nothing, because Potter didn't look. A person can pout a long, long time.

On the third day the Oriole scolded him. 'Pish, Potter, here is a blockhead for you! The very thing I brought you to see is now before you. The wonder of God is on two legs and his mercy is here in the flesh, and the birds who miss it count themselves unlucky, and that is the most of the birds—but you! You come and stick your nose in your armpit! You mope and miss it. You feel sorry for yourself and so you mock the gift of God. Potter, Potter, the Phoenix is alive again! That's what he comes to show us every half one thousand years, and this is the wonderful end of the story in our own seeing, so that we know, so that we believe it, so that we have hope past our dying. Look at him, Potter! The dead, they do not die forever. Nay! They rise again! Birds by the Phoenix, boys by the love of God. Look, Potter, look at the Phoenix. Let the blockhead see and believe.'

Indeed, something was different in the world, thought Potter. What it was, it sounded different. Distant noises were gathering, tiny chirps and whistlings, twitters, hoots and downright crows, cackles, cries and lonely scolds, and warbling—

Potter peeped out from under his wing. Behind him, still, was the wide wilderness. But in front of him, high in the top of the tallest palm, stood the Phoenix once again, so beautiful, shaking ash from his royal feathers, young, so young, so strong and free from suffering!

Out of his ashes? whispered Potter. The same love and the same fear kicked at his heart for the sight of the marvellous bird, but harder now since he never thought to see him again.

'Out of his ashes,' said the Oriole.

You, Felix! cried Potter, gazing at the eagle eye and ready to burst into tears all over again, but this time for joy. *Oh, you Felix!* he shrieked. *How much I love you!*

Potter wanted to fly up into the air. Potter clung to his branch, afraid to lose the vision, because look! Look at the force in the hunch of his shoulders, oh! Look at his glorious crown. And look how he spreads his wings a twelve-foot span, how he slides from the palm, how he strokes and caresses the wind. Oh, look how the thunderbird goes rising up!

Potter began to giggle. He whooped and he plain laughed. His belly tickled at the sight, as though a mountain had kissed him and then had flown. He let go his branch, and without another thought he shot after the Phoenix, higher and higher, and eastward.

Oh, Felix! There was nothing wiser in all the world to do, than to follow the Phoenix eastward. Nobody asked, 'Is this right?' They simply did it.

They? They, by the thousands. Birds by the tens of thousands, singing the songs that Potter had heard at a distance. Potter had company!

Out of the green, across the wilderness they came in a rushing multitude, every family and feather, a great cloud of witnesses, a skyborne jubilation! Pigeons and eagles and sparrows flitting; hawks and swallows and geese; thrashers, kingfishers, terns, the shrikes and the crow; tanagers, warblers, larks and the loon, and here and there a dumpy chicken given flight; starlings in overwhelming population; robins, wrens, and cuckoos; pheasant, partridge, turkeys, buzzards, vultures and the owl—a wonderful company, so thick as to darken the earth, and laughing all as Potter laughed, delighted by their holiday, and no one pecking another one. No, these were at noisy peace together. They flew with the joy of life, life not overcome by death. The story had happened again: the Phoenix was their hope, and all their song was 'Hallelujah!'

Eastward, eastward sailed the Phoenix. Eastward Potter,

too, with never the question *Where are we going?* It didn't matter. He laughed with his friend the Oriole, that was all.

But this day had its ending, too.

For at evening the mighty Phoenix headed into a high and holy wind. It was a good wind, carrying strange and tasty smells and boiling with unearthly colour. They did not hate the wind. But it was also a wind of absolute denial, for it blew harder than any bird could fly. Soon ten thousand birds, each beating as quick as it could, stood perfectly still in the sky, while the Phoenix flew on alone.

Where is he going? cried Potter, the screaming wind in his ears.

'Back,' called the Oriole. 'Back to Paradise, where death can never be, nor tears, nor pain, nor crying any more.'

Can't I go with him?

'Potter, you haven't finished dying yet.'

I will miss him.

'But you will remember him,' cried the Oriole. Both were cutting the violent current.

Suddenly Potter caught sight of a final wonder. One tiny blackbird was drawn into the slipstream behind the Phoenix and followed close at his back. When the Phoenix was swallowed by the lovely cloud, so was this bird sucked in— and there was a flash of red at its shoulder.

Then the wind and the cloud together passed away, and all of the birds were left in a nowhere.

Did you see that? asked Potter.

'Aye,' said the Oriole. 'I did.'

Somebody entered Paradise!

'Aye. Somebody done with dying.'

Oh, Baltimore Oriole! Who is so lucky to be with dear Felix forever?

They were floating, now, on an easy wind, the two of them alone, facing westward and the deep green of the evening.

The Oriole said, 'What colour did that blackbird wear?'

Potter said, *Red.*

The Oriole said, 'And what was the colour of your friend Jonathan?'

Potter smiled. Potter grew thoughtful and older at once. Potter flew on with knowing strokes of the wing. But Potter never answered, because he didn't have to any more.

He didn't say, *Red.*

'Fly home, Potter. Fly home as fast as you can.'

The song of the Baltimore Oriole had changed. Now it was an urgent pleading and no nonsense: the wonderful story was done, the evening begun. There were important matters of the world to remember, now.

'Fly home.'

But I want to stay with the birds, said Potter.

'You are not a bird,' said the Oriole.

Feathers! cried Potter. *And flight at the rim of the sky! That's not a bird? And I flew with Felix—*

'Soul of a boy, you are not a bird,' said the Oriole.

They were over the sea, two purple specks far behind the westering chariot of the sun.

'And besides all that,' said the Oriole, 'your mother thinks that you are dead.'

Look at me! cried Potter. *I am not dead!*

And to prove it he slipped waterward, a happy dive. He skimmed spume from the ocean till his belly and his balled claws were wet. He soared aloft, performing barrel rolls of magnificent spiral through the air, during all of which the Oriole flew straight forward and no nonsense.

'Potter!' the Oriole called sharply, 'you have seen what love is. Now love!'

Then that bird took speed and shot forward in an earnest flight, so that Potter had to cease his foolishness and fly hard in order to catch up.

'Your mother,' said the Oriole, 'is sad. She is weeping.'

Weeping? Crying? said Potter.

'With all of her heart. For you.'

For me? Potter asked.

'And why not? She thinks that you are dead, and she loves you, and who's to tell her otherwise but you?'

But I'm not dead!

'So tell her, Potter. Comfort her. Now is the time to share the resurrection. Or would you keep such a wonder to yourself?'

No. Suddenly Potter was worried for his mother, and his heart raced.

'Fly home, Potter. Fly home as fast as you can.'

But here came the night behind them. Here came the darkness at celestial speeds, for the sun was so far ahead. Oh, day and night turned faster than wheels on a railroad track, and Potter felt so slow. The night would beat him home. The night would grieve his mother, if he were found dead forever—

Baltimore Oriole, he cried, *how can we fly faster than the night?*

Two dots darting, two birds busy with their wings, two friends, they swooped and sank as God gave them strength. And nobody saw them go. Neither the people below nor the angels above thought anything wonderful in their flight— because who knew the glory they had seen? Who knew it was the soul of a boy midocean and midair? Who knew he went to comfort his mother?

Across the country they sped. The chariot of the sun had long since disappeared. *Wait for us!* cried Potter. *My mother does not understand!* But the sun kept his own schedule. Night had caught up with them, and the air was cold, and Potter was shivering, and darkness lay on the face of the earth. The lights of cities looked like a yellow rash. Rivers were black serpents waiting. Lakes were inky deeps. How lonely was all the land in shadows! How lost its peoples!

Ma-AH-ma! Ma! Ma! wailed Potter. He was so saddened by what he saw after the blazing wonder of the east. And in so vast a territory, how would he find his mother again? *Ma-AH-ma! Ma! Ma!*

'There!' called the Oriole, and he dropped straight down.

Down, too, went Potter, toward the edge of one river, circling round and round until a large two-storey house was at the centre of his circlings, and the window therein was his own.

'Friends,' said the Oriole.

Potter barely heard him. For when he perched on the ledge outside his window and peered inside, his heart broke for the sight before him.

Dim light was in his bedroom. On the bed lay the body of a boy, his mouth wide open as if screaming, but his eyes were closed, and the corpse wore only underpants, and Potter was ashamed. Next to the bed, kneeling, was his mother. Her hands were spread on Potter's chest. Her face was in the sheets. She was crying, crying, shaking her shoulders. And his father stood with his forehead against the wall, and he was crying, too.

Poppi! Who could stand to see his father cry? *Oh, please dear Baltimore Oriole, tell my parents that it is all okay—*

But he heard no answer at his side. Only the wind. The Oriole had gone. Everywhere, over all the lonely world, it was night.

Mama! You shouldn't cry! called Potter. *I am alive!*

At that same moment, his father made a fist. Like a hammer he brought his fist against the wall, once, twice, three times. And then the strong man turned and sank beside the bed of his boy and wailed, 'Potter!' and that stabbed Potter to the heart.

He began to beat his wings. He cried *Oooooooo* like a dove. He scratched the broken glass. His father heard the commotion, leaped up and lunged for the window. He threw up the sash and roared, 'Go away!' Poor Potter fluttered backward. Then his father ran from the room, and a great pounding began in the depths of the house.

Potter landed on the ledge again. His mother raised her grieving face and said, 'Please go away. He can't stand to see birds now—'

But it's me, wailed Potter. *It's only me!*

His father returned with a broom handle. This he thrust out into the night, and he waved it, trying to hit Potter. *Poppi!* 'Haven't you done enough?' roared his father. 'My son Potter was the best boy that a man could have! Wicked birds! I loved him!' All at once the man sagged on the windowsill, and the broom handle slipped to the bushes below, and he simply wept. 'God is my witness,' he wept, 'how I loved the boy.'

Don't, don't, Poppi, don't, cried Potter. He was weeping, too.

Then Potter's mother came to the side of the man, and she knelt down, and she put her arms around him, and she said, 'Hush, Papa, hush. The birds could not take our son from us. What do the birds have to do with it? Hush, now. Hush.'

They put their faces together, his mother and his father, holding one another. That was Potter's chance. On muffled wings, like the owl, Potter sailed into the bedroom over their heads and landed by the body of the boy. As swiftly as he could, he crammed himself into the open mouth, a cold cave waiting, and he crawled down the throat in such a hurry that he caused a tickling there.

The boy began to cough.

But behold: he was laughing, too.

Coughing and laughing together, the tears filling up his eyes, and watching the faces of his father and his mother, Potter choked, 'No, no! But you must love the birds—' That was all he could say. The cough took hold of him and twisted his body all over the bed, and he barked, and he grew pink.

So his father rushed to him, grabbed him, lifted him with a loud shout and squeezed him so that it seemed that his bones would crack.

'Potter, Potter, O Potter!' his father cried with his face to the ceiling. 'We thought you broke the window to fly, to go the way that Jonathan had gone. We thought—O my son, my son, Potter!'

The boy felt whiskers deep in his neck and strong arms all around him. He wanted to tell them that the birds praise God, and Jonathan is just fine, and—But he could only cough: the Unstoppable Cough, Potter called it.

His mother was the wise one. His mother had the eyes of understanding. She said, 'He did, Martin. He went away. But what does it matter now? He came back to us again.' She pushed the hair from Potter's forehead. 'And I think you chose to come home, didn't you, Potter?'

Branta and the
Golden Stone

*O*nce there was a girl who lived alone on the northernmost island in all the world.

She lived in a cottage by a lake. The lake was ice for most of the year, banked with snow. Her father had built the cottage long ago. It had two rooms and a fireplace, a table, a chair, a little window that faced the lake, and in each room a little bed.

The girl had flashing black eyes and midnight hair tied back from her brow. Her neck was noble, her skin so dark it gleamed in the moonlight—and always she wore a snow-white scarf buttoned above her ears.

If she walked abroad in the snow, you could see her because of her dark skin.

If she walked abroad at night, you could see her because of her scarf.

Her name was Branta.

And often that winter she walked abroad. She left the cottage and wandered across the frozen lake exactly as the moon goes wandering across the sky. Branta was lonely.

Her father had died a year ago.

He had been a big man once, with a wild white beard and tremendous arms for carrying firewood. Branta's father had always kept a fire in the fireplace. No matter how cold the winter grew, their cottage was warm and bright and lovely.

But then one morning the man didn't get out of bed.

Branta had knocked on his door. 'Papa?' she whispered.

'Papa?' But all she heard was a moaning like wind in the trees. She opened the door and saw by his eyes that her father was very sick.

All day long she bathed his face. He seemed to be sleeping. He seemed to be fighting inside his dreams. For her father's sake, Branta kept the fire bright and warm in the fireplace.

Then in the evening he called to her. 'Branta.'

'What, Papa?'

'Sit beside me,' he whispered. 'I have something to tell you.'

She sat and bent her noble neck toward him. He closed his eyes and spoke.

'You've never asked why we live so far north,' he said.

'I never minded,' said Branta.

'Once,' said the man with the wild white beard, 'when your mother and I were young and happy, I was a *magus*— a wise man—Branta. I could read the stars in heaven as if they were words on a page. But then,' he whispered very softly, 'I stole the Golden Stone, and it made me famous. It made me more than a *magus*. It made me a magician.'

'Papa?' said Branta. 'Why didn't you tell me these things before?'

He opened his eyes and looked at his daughter. 'Because I am ashamed of them,' he said. 'They made your mother sad.'

'But then why are you telling me now?'

'Because I must give you something before I die,' he said, 'and you must understand it.'

'Die?' said Branta. 'Oh, Papa, let's talk of other things. Here, let me go build the fire for you—'

'No, let the fire grow cold!' her father commanded. 'Stay with me and listen!'

Far, far into the night then, while the fire dwindled to ash and the grey ash cooled, Branta's father told her his story.

'The most important message I ever read in the stars,' he said, 'was that a Baby King was to be born in a distant kingdom. When I told it to your mother, she said, "Go. Who else can read the stars as you do? Who else knows that the Baby King is coming? Yet someone must welcome him. Go."

'So my brothers took spices from orient trees as gifts, and I took a stone of gold for the Baby King. We travelled the deserts westward. Finally, we found the tiny child, and I knew at once he was more than a baby and more than a king.

'He gazed at us from his mother's arms. He raised his hands and blessed us. My brothers put their spices on the ground before him, but I lifted my gift to the child himself. He reached and touched it. Branta, listen: Where his finger touched the gold it made a deep print; and the whole stone glowed hot in my hand, and I felt power go into it!

'Branta, Branta, I never let go of that stone. And when no one was looking, I slipped it into my pouch. My brothers brought frankincense and myrrh and left them there. I brought gold and took it back again. I stole the Golden Stone and the print of the Baby King's finger.'

Tears flowed from the old man's eyes now, but he kept on talking.

'Your mother was frightened when she saw what I had done. "Take it back," she said. "It belongs to the Baby King!"

'I said, "But if the Good King touched it, it will do good for many people."

'She said, "Please, please, take it back."

'But I didn't. I used it. And, indeed, I did much good with it. For this was the power of the Golden Stone, that it changed people. It made them whatever they wanted to be. It made sick people healthy, it gave sight to the blind, it caused the crippled to walk. And often I said to your mother, "Do you see all the good I'm doing?"

'But she said, "No, husband. I see instead that the Golden Stone has changed you, too. Now you are what you always wanted to be, a magician proud and famous. And that is not good."

'Your mother's words made me angry. So I said, "Woman, be still!"

'She looked at me and said, "Do you mean that?"

' "Shut up! Shut up!" I shouted. "Woman, don't talk to me!"

'Well, then your mother went to the place where I kept the Golden Stone. She put her finger on the Baby King's print, and she whispered, "You have your wish. It is my wish, too. I will never speak again."

'In the days that followed, your mother did not speak, and I continued my work with the Golden Stone. People came and were changed.

'Did an angry man want to be fire to burn his enemy's house? When he left he was a pure white flame, and his enemy's house burned down, indeed—but the man himself was never seen again.

'Did a greedy man wish to be rain to get himself rich crops? Well, he became a wonderful rainstorm, and his fields brought forth abundantly—but someone else harvested them, because this man had run in streams to the sea.

'Do you hear the danger of the Golden Stone, Branta?' the old man asked. 'No, no, it wasn't all goodness. Whatever the people became, they had to stay that way forever. If someone wished silence for a little while—well, the silence lasted forever. Is the fire out yet,' he whispered. 'Is the grating cold yet?'

Quietly, Branta rose and went to the fireplace. 'Yes,' she said. 'It is out.'

'Your mother died in silence,' the man said. Branta could not see him in the darkness. It sounded as if he were speaking from far away. 'She was going to have a baby. She lay down in silence. In silence she bore a baby girl. And in silence she died. Branta, you were that baby girl.

'Branta?' the old man called. 'Branta, can you hear me?'

But she could not speak now, because of her sadness. She could only nod.

Her father said, 'Reach into the ashes. Do you feel something hard and smooth?'

Yes, she felt a stone the size of a sparrow's egg.

'Please bring it here,' he said, and Branta did. She carried to her father a stone of gold so pure it glowed upon their faces. In its centre was a baby's fingerprint.

'When your mother died, I tried to find the King to return his stone,' the old man whispered. 'But that was years later, and no one knew of such a king. So I went away. I brought us to the northernmost island in the world, and I built a little

86

cottage, and I built a big fire to keep you warm, and I loved you, child, and I tried…' The old man closed his eyes.

Branta waited for him to draw his next breath, but he never did. Her father's beard was like the night cloud round his face. He was peaceful now, and he was dead.

So that's why Branta lived alone by the lake. And that's why she walked abroad all winter long in loneliness. She was thinking about her father.

When the nights were still, she would button the white scarf above her ears and go forth like the moon. When blizzards struck her island, blowing and shrieking and piling snow against the cottage, she stayed inside, building fires bright and warm.

But every night, whether windy or still, she would touch the Golden Stone, which now she kept in the centre of her father's pillow as a memorial to him.

The northernmost island in all the world is winter for most of the year. But finally there comes a brief spring when the ice breaks and the water gurgles down to the lake and the flowers sprout and grow.

And so it was that the winter of Branta's sadness suddenly came to an end when company came to her island awhile.

One morning, while the water still dripped from the eaves of her cottage, Branta stepped outside and looked around. She thought she'd heard somebody laughing.

The lake was glittering, the hills were green, the sky was bright and perfectly blue; but there was nobody anywhere, nobody laughing—

All at once she heard it again. Straight up in the sky so high they were invisible, *two* somebodies were chatting and laughing and telling jokes in nasal voices: '*Gaba-gaba-gaba!*' they said.

'Who are you?' Branta cried.

And then, exactly as if in answer to her question, she saw in the distance two dark bodies with points in front and streaks at their sides, which Branta took to be wings.

'Birds,' she whispered.

They began to spiral down toward her island, great birds with black faces and long necks, pure white markings at their throats, grey bodies, and wings of a powerful stroke.

'Why, you are geese!' cried Branta, and she raised her hands for gladness. 'Geese! Geese, I hope you will land on my lake!'

And they did!

Down they sailed on outstretched wings—splendid, regal creatures. They made a circle over the water, then pulled up on the flap of a wing, bent their necks, put out their feet, skated the surface, and sank and sat and twitched their tails, curving their noble necks. A long journey was done.

'Geese!' cried Branta. 'Geese, tell me a joke and I will laugh with you!'

But the goose and her gander only glanced once at the girl on the shore; then they paddled to the other side of the lake, where they chatted and groomed their feathers.

'*Gaba-gaba-gaba,*' they said—no language Branta could understand, no joke that she could laugh at. For geese are geese and people are people. They can be neighbours sharing a lake, but they cannot talk or hug as fathers and daughters do.

'But you don't mind if I watch you, do you?' Branta murmured.

Gaba-gaba-gaba. From their distance, the geese didn't seem to mind at all.

Branta took comfort in that. Life had returned to her island. And so the summer was good to her, and she was glad.

Flowers burst in red and blue. The grass grew long all around the lake. The female goose made a nest in the tall green shade, and in her nest she laid six eggs; and the gander and she made comfortable cluckings both day and night, and Branta was filled with excitement. In all her life she had never seen babies before.

So then the eggs hatched. And here came six brave goslings, each a puffball the size of Branta's fist, all following their mother, peeping, charging the waves of the lake, and rowing out like tiny boats.

Branta laughed aloud on the shore, and sometimes the baby geese glanced in her direction, and then she laughed harder than ever—as if she had the right to feel proud of such handsome babies.

But swiftly do babies grow up. Soon the goslings were gone and six true geese had taken their places, six faces black-and-white, six necks as noble as their parents' necks, six pairs of wings now strong for flight, and six new voices calling '*Gaba-gaba-gaba*' in laughter Branta could not join, in language she couldn't understand.

The summer was over. Eight grown geese would soon depart. Branta began to prepare for winter, carrying firewood into the cottage as her father had done before her and stiffening her heart for the loneliness soon to come again.

But this was the northernmost island in all the world. Winter can come here so suddenly that even geese might be caught by surprise.

In the year after Branta's father died, that is exactly what happened. One night summer died. A storm tore down from the northern seas and beat against her cottage all night long.

When she crept to her window in the morning, Branta saw that the grass was broken and frozen in ice, the sky was low and blowing, and the lake had been lashed to a foaming black fury. The north wind blew and blew—and there, huddled behind a boulder bigger than they, were the geese!

'Oh, no!' cried Branta. 'I thought you were gone! Dear geese, you can hardly walk in this weather—however will you fly?'

All day Branta watched the family from her window, but the wind didn't break and the geese didn't move. And then the night arrived in perfect darkness, and the wind blew so fiercely that the fire in her fireplace cowered and guttered out.

On the second day of the storm it snowed. The lake stayed black; but the ground grew thick with drifts, and the geese were swallowed altogether.

'Where are you?' Branta called. She buttoned the white scarf above her ears and ran out into the blizzard. 'Are you dead?' She stumbled toward the boulder, which was now sunken in snow. 'Please, please,' she cried, 'don't die!'

Branta reached into the snowdrift and touched warm feathers. Immediately, eight geese burst up in a shower of snow and began to race away from her. Branta chased them.

'Wait,' she called. 'I want to help you!'

But they were afraid of her! They were as scared of Branta as they were of the storm. When she ran at the gander, he opened his wings to fly from her; but the wind slapped him backward, and he rolled like a snowball along the ground. She tried to grab him. 'Come with me,' she begged. 'You'll die out here.'

But it was no good. The gander stuck his face in the wind and with a desperate beating of his wings moved farther and farther away. So did they all. Branta had visions of eight geese frozen in the cold, their black eyes closed or clouded. Yet whenever she drew near to them, they ran faster and farther away.

So then, thought Branta, *maybe I could scare them into the cottage!* She began to wave her arms and to scream louder than the wind. 'Go! Go! Go!' she screamed—and for a little while the plan worked. The geese ran in front of her. She aimed them toward the door of her cottage, the warmth of the fire—

But at the last instant they split and raced around the cottage, farther and farther away.

'Oh, you stupid geese!' Branta wept. She stopped and leaned against the cottage wall. 'You have to come inside. The cold is going to kill you, don't you know?' What could she possibly do to save them?

'*Gaba-gaba-gaba!*' said the gander. And then, no matter how tired his family was, no matter how windy the world or how cold, they gathered all around him. '*Gaba-gaba-gaba,*' he said—and suddenly Branta knew exactly what she would do.

She walked into the cottage. She knelt before the fire to be sure there was plenty of wood to last a long, long time. Then she rose and went into her father's room.

At his bedside she reached for the Golden Stone still on his pillow, and she held it in the palm of her hand awhile, gazing at the tiny fingerprint.

'Baby King,' she said, 'I want to be a goose.'

Branta placed the Golden Stone on her tongue. It was small. It tasted like spices, bitter and sweet and powerful.

Then she swallowed it.

For a moment she kept her head bowed in silence. Then a fire rose in her heart, which became a blazing brand. It coursed through her veins to the surface of her flesh, and she bent down, she bent her long neck down—and when she raised it up again, Branta was a goose, a bright and glowing goose, for the heat went out from her body into the air.

Now she went back the way that she had come. She took short steps, silly, waddling steps, out into the storm—but the cold did not sting her anymore. She walked through drifts to the back of the cottage, calling '*Gaba-gaba-gaba!*' Here and there various geese poked their heads up through the snow, looking for the source of the cry.

'*Gather-gather-gather*,' called Branta the goose, nipping the younger geese on the backs of their necks. Some of them had already tucked their heads beneath their wings, preparing to sleep and to die. Branta would not allow it. '*Gaba-gaba-get up!*' she scolded them.

The mother of the children was staring into the darkness, nearly dead with cold. But when she saw Branta—somebody exactly her size and shape, with the same white markings under her throat and the same black beak—well, she stood up and followed. Of course! Why wouldn't one goose trust and follow another goose who spoke the exact same language, after all?

And the gander said, '*Gaba-gaba-Branta!*' He called her by name. '*Good-for-you-ba-Branta,*' he said, and then he was the last of the family of geese to follow her into the cottage; and there they all spent the third night of the storm, close to a fire both warm and bright. And so it was that they survived.

When finally the storm abated that year and the sun returned to warm the earth awhile, a flock of geese flew up from the northernmost island in all the world. They formed a perfect V and turned toward the south. It was late in the season to be leaving, but these geese were no less healthy nor strong for that.

Soon they were gossiping and telling jokes. Soon they were laughing, as do all geese when they travel.

'*Gaba-gaba-gaba!*' they said.

There were nine in the flock: six children flying their first flight south, a mother goose and a gander, too—and one that had once been a girl, Branta, laughing as freely as any goose.

For this was the truth of the Golden Stone, the length of love and the fullness of sacrifice: that whatever a person chose to become, she would stay that way forever.

Thistle

*O*nce upon a time there lived a man and a woman in a potato house. The house wasn't made of potatoes. It was called the potato house because that's what the good man did. That was his work. He grew potatoes.

All day long, every day of the summer, he went to the fields and ploughed and planted. He weeded and watered potato bushes. And when the leaves turned brown, he dug in the earth—he dug to the roots where potatoes grow and pulled out bushels and bushels for people to eat.

But every day too, exactly at noon, the man went back to his house, threw open the door and hollered, 'I'm hungry! Good wife, I am hungry and ready to eat. Let's have potatoes!'

It was a happy life, and they were happy people. There was only one thing that made them sad. They had no children. In the afternoons when he weeded the fields and she made soup in the kitchen, the man and the woman felt lonely for children.

So every night they folded their hands and prayed, 'Dear God, do you think we could have a baby or two?'

And very soon, they did.

They had a son.

Ah, he was a tall lad! He stood like a tree, slender, straight and proud, his head thrown back, his nose on high, his eyes as green as needles. The man and the woman called him Pine, and they smiled because a family of two plus one is three.

Soon they had another son. This boy was very strong. His legs were like two trunks, his back like the bark of a mighty tree, his arms all hard with muscle. So the man and the woman called him Oak, and they laughed because three plus one is four.

Again God answered their prayer, and here came a daughter so pretty her parents got tears just looking at her. Her skin was like petals, pale and pink. The blush on her cheek was red and rare. And her neck was a tender, bending flower stalk. So they called her Rose, and they wept for gladness. Four plus one is five, and five is such a lovely number.

Then one more baby was born in the potato house. A girl. Not tall, she was short. Not strong, she was round and chubby, clumsy and soft. And plain. This child was as plain as a window weed. The man and the woman loved her very much, but because they were an honest couple they named her Thistle, and they said to God, 'Six is a nice number. Six is enough.'

So six is where the family stopped, and the man and the woman were lonely no longer. They were smiling. They were happy.

That is, they were happy most of the time—but not when Thistle cried. It broke their hearts when the youngest one cried. And every day, just as the man went out to work in the fields, little Thistle covered her eyes and cried.

Pine said, 'Shortness, Shortness, why are you crying?'

Oak said, 'She can't help it. Fatness always cries.'

'Oh, Thistle!' said Rose. 'Can you do nothing but cry?'

But the woman frowned at her older children and took the

little one on her lap and whispered, 'Thistle, what is the matter?'

Thistle said, 'Papa is gone. I miss my papa.'

'So that's the reason you are sad,' the good woman said. 'Well, wait a while and he will be home again.'

And soon he was home indeed. Exactly at noon, every noon of the year, the good man stood in the doorway and hollered, 'I'm hungry! Family, I'm hungry and ready to eat. Let's have potatoes!'

Now it happened one morning that, while he was digging potatoes with a sharp new shovel, the good man heard a groaning under the ground.

'Mmmmmm.'

He got down on his knees and listened. 'Mmmmmm.' He began to dig the earth with his bare hands—and soon he felt a potato, a huge potato, a tuber bigger than any he'd ever met before.

The more he dug, the more he saw. It had rough skin and eyes all over and lumps, one lump on each side and two lumps like legs at the end of it. But this particular potato was enormous! It was twice the size of the man himself.

Suddenly one of its eyes popped open and stared straight at the man.

The man jumped backward. He had never been stared at by a potato before.

The four lumps jerked and started to move. Like arms and legs they kicked the dirt, and the giant potato climbed out of the hole and stood up! Other eyes blinked and opened. A thousand potato eyes rolled around until they were all glaring at the poor man, who was so frightened that he couldn't move.

Then the potato began to talk.

'My name is Pudge!' it roared. 'And hungry!' it thundered. 'I'm hungry, hungry, and ready to eat!' Oh, what a horrible roaring it made, as thick as brown gravy. 'And here is my dinner before me,' Pudge bellowed. 'Man, I'm going to eat you!'

So that is exactly what Pudge the potato did: ate the good man, shoes, shovel and all.

Then up on bumpish legs Pudge walked to the good man's house. Exactly at noon the huge potato kicked open the door and roared, 'I'm hungry!'

Inside the house was the man's whole family, his wife and all his children.

'My name is Pudge,' Pudge bellowed. 'I'm hungry, hungry, and ready to eat. And, Woman, I'm going to eat you!'

Which is what Pudge did—swallowed the woman completely down, then turned and stomped away.

So there stood Pine perpendicular, and Oak so muscle-bound, and Rose in a pretty faint—and Thistle. Four children all alone in the potato house, and the youngest one was crying.

'Oh, Thistle,' said Pine, 'can you do nothing but cry? No, nothing but cry.'

Then he drew himself up straight and proud. 'I,' he said, 'I am the oldest. I am also the tallest and the smartest. Therefore it is my job to save us. I am going out into the wide world to find some weapon for fighting the ugly Pudge, and we will be right after all.'

Oak slapped his brother on the back. Rose praised him prettily. And Thistle cried. 'I will miss you, Pine,' she said.

Pine said, 'Hush! I'll be back soon enough.' And he left.

For a long, long time Pine travelled the wide world. He strode down country roads. He followed trails through the tangled woods. He looked high and low and here and there, seeking some weapon with which to fight Pudge, some magical something—but he could find nothing at all.

Then through the trees he noticed an ancient Beldame sitting on a stump. She was a hideous thing! So hunched was she that her knees reached over her ears. Her nose stuck out ten inches in front of her face, all covered with warts and dripping. Her chin stuck out ten inches too, hairy and covered with drool—and the tips of nose and chin touched like a scissors when she talked. There were exactly three grey hairs on the top of her bald head. Worst of all, she was smiling!

So ugly was the Beldame that Pine planned to pass her staring at the sky and whistling, pretending that there were no ancient Beldames anywhere in sight.

But she raised an arm as skinny as sticks, and she spoke.

'Handsome lad,' she croaked, her nose and her chin snapping together, 'where be thee going?'

'Madame, no business of yours,' Pine said without stopping.

'Ahhh!' the Beldame cried, 'I can read the green of thine eye, lad. 'Tis a weapon thou seekest! For 'twas a Pudge did gobble thy father down and thy mother too, and now thou art bound to fight a Pudge thyself.'

Pine paused at such knowledge. Pine stopped altogether,

looked down on oldness as bent as a toad, and said, 'So?'

'So, lad—so, laddy,' the Beldame cried, 'I can give thee such weapons as will make a potato's tummy ache.'

'Right!' said Pine, stretching forth his hand. 'Give and I'll be gone, hag.'

'Whisht! Not so hasty!' the Beldame screeched, grinning. 'We'll make a trade of it,' she said. 'First let me give thee something that pleasures me, and *then* will I give thee the weapons, too.'

'What can please a hag as old as you?' Pine asked.

'Why, kisses, lad!' screamed the Beldame. 'Ten kisses from these wrinkled lips. 'Tis a nose and a chin have stopped my sweetest kissing, and never may I kiss again except some kind child be willing to receive it. Aye,' the Beldame whispered, 'but I have been so lonely so long. Green Eyes, let me kiss thee.'

Well, Pine didn't even think about her trade. He drew himself up to his most splendid height, extended his long arm downward, and said, 'I'll take the weapons, thank you. As for the kisses, keep them. How could I put my handsomeness between a warty nose and a slippery chin?'

The ancient Beldame fell silent. Down went her head between her knees, down, down as low as the stump. Thin went her eyes, as thin as whips. She smiled a sort of thorny smile, and softly she began to sing:

> 'Then take thee, Pine, what is thy due,
> A clutch of weapons fit for you:
> No bow nor blade nor studded boots.
> No need of these—*thou shalt have roots!*'

Roots, thought Pine. Good! Anything given to one as smart as he must surely be worthy, fine weapons for fighting Pudge.

Home, then, he ran at very high speeds.

Nobly he took a stand inside the potato house. Taller and prouder than ever was he, his eyes bright green with excitement, for he was about to fight the most glorious fight of all.

He stood facing the door, waiting, waiting. His brother and sisters crouched behind him. Exactly at noon the door flew open, and there was Pudge, a thousand eyes a-blazing.

Pine threw back his head and raised his arms, ready to learn what sort of weapons *roots* might be, ready to attack.

'My name is Pudge!' the potato bellowed. 'I'm hungry, hungry, and ready to eat! And, Toothpick, I'm going to eat you!'

Pine tried to jump at Pudge. But he couldn't. He tried to run, but he couldn't do that either. He was absolutely fixed to the floor. By *roots*!

So Pudge rolled forward to the poor, immobile Pine, opened a monstrous maw and swallowed the fellow down, then turned and stomped away.

Take two from six and four is left. And one from four is three. Now there were only three children left in the potato house, and one of these was crying.

'Hush, Thistle, hush!' said Oak. 'Can you do nothing but cry?'

And Rose said, 'No, nothing but cry.'

'But I never cry,' said Oak to his sisters. 'And I am strong, the strongest of all,' he said. 'A man of few words, a man of action am I. Therefore, girls, I'm off to find the weapon Pine could not.'

'Oak!' Thistle called. 'Oak, I will miss you.'

Too late. He was already gone, marching abroad as if he were an entire army, barking the steps as he went: 'Hut, two, three, four! Hut, two, three, four!'

As it happened, Oak followed the same route Pine had taken. Soon, then, he was passing the ancient Beldame on her stump, who dripped from the tip of her nose, who drooled at her chin.

'Strong swain!' she cried. 'Where be thee going so mighty and sure?'

'To war,' Oak shouted, 'two, three, four!'

'What!' screamed the Beldame. 'Is the world at war and I knew it not?'

'Tut-tut, Elder! No need to know what doesn't concern you. I go to gain a victory. I lack but the weapons to do it.'

'Weapons, weapons, the world wants weapons,' muttered the Beldame, 'whereas I sit here full of the cunningest weapons for cutting Pudges to bits...'

'Pudges?' cried Oak. He stopped and faced the skinny Beldame. 'Did you say Pudges?'

'The sort of Pudges as gobble people. Aye.'

'Well,' said Oak, 'give me your weapons and I'll leave you in peace. I'm a man of action and very few words!'

'And 'tis action I seek,' yelled the Beldame. 'Prithee, brave soldier, let's come to terms—a thing for a thing between us. Let me give thee what pleasures me, and then I'll give what thou needest.'

'Whatever,' Oak said.

'Ahhh!' shrieked the ancient Beldame. 'He saith *whatever*! A generous answer, that.'

'Terms, Elder! Tell me your terms and I'll go.'

Slowly and sweetly she whispered, 'To kiss thee.'

'What?'

'Aye, I long to be less lonely. To find one soldier brave enough to brush these withered lips. To give thee, sir, five kisses only, after which I'll give thee such wonderful weapons…'

Oak made a fist and pounded his chest. 'I am a fighter, not a lover!' he shouted. 'Forget about kisses. Give me weapons!'

Once again the Beldame's head sank down until her two knees touched above it. Her eyes grew sharper than knives. Her cheeks went white. She smiled a freezing smile and began to sing this little song:

> 'Snakes and serpents, adders, newts—
> For all thy muscles, substitutes!
> I'll send thee, soldier,
> Home the bolder:
> Strong, strong Oak, *Thou shalt have roots!*'

'HUT-TWO-THREE-FOUR!HUTTWOTHREE FOUR…'

Right away, Oak was galloping back to the potato house, counting the steps and whooping as he went. 'Roots? Roots?

Whatever!' he cried. 'Soldiers can fight with any weapon!'

He pushed his sisters out of the way and stood foursquare before the door.

BOOM! The door flew open. The monstrous potato was here.

'My name is Pudge!' Pudge bellowed. 'I'm hungry, hungry, and ready to eat! And, Acorn, I'm going to eat you!'

If Oak was strong, then roots were stronger. They held the poor boy so fast to the floor that he could neither run nor fight. Instead, he was swallowed, and the great Pudge turned and stomped away.

One from three leaves two. Two sisters alone were left in the potato house, and one of these was crying.

'Oh, Thistle,' Rose scolded, 'can you do nothing but cry? No, nothing but cry. I, on the other hand, have a plan. Thistle,' she said, 'do you see how beautiful I am?'

Thistle nodded. No one could help but see how beautiful Rose was.

'Well, beauty is better than muscles or brains because beauty can turn the foe against himself! Wait here,' said Rose. 'I'll be back in a bit.'

'Rose, I will miss you,' poor Thistle cried.

But Rose was already gone. Skipping lightly, humming a silly tune, she was travelling through the world, and soon, just like her brothers before her, she saw the ancient Beldame crouched on a stump.

For just a moment she was shocked to find so much ugliness in one spare body.

But then she took control of herself and stared straight ahead with icy eyes, waiting for the Beldame to notice the difference between the two of them and be properly ashamed.

The Beldame, however, knew no shame. Neither did she spend time chatting with this particular child. Bluntly she croaked the terms of her trade: 'Weapons for kisses, my pretty,' she said. 'Let me give thee but a single kiss, and then I shall dress thee in wonderful weapons.'

Rose was not surprised by the request. The stones themselves would kiss her if they had lips and she gave them permission.

But she tossed her head and said, 'Those who someday kiss me will be worthy of the favour. That's one or two, just one or two in all the world. And you,' Rose sniffed, 'are not among them.'

The ancient Beldame nodded and nodded as if this were a pretty saying, suitable for remembering. But so low did her old head go this time, that her chin was scratching the ground. So slitty were her eyes that they could have cut. And so softly did the Beldame sing, that Rose could scarcely hear the song:

> 'The Rose that loves the rosebud best
> Deserves what I gave all the rest;
> Dost love thy form? Thy stem? Thy shoots?
> Take one thing more: *Thou shalt have roots!*'

Rose neither blinked nor blanched. She shrugged and said, 'My brothers never knew what to do with your gift.

Roots, is it? Well, I will take your evil and make it my good.'

The ancient Beldame closed her eyes with a smile as bleak as winter.

But Rose tripped lightly home again, told Thistle to keep to her place, then turned to wait for Pudge.

Exactly at noon the door flew open, and there was Pudge gazing with a thousand eyes at the lovely and limpid Rose.

'Sugar!' Pudge bellowed. 'I'm hungry, hungry, and ready to eat... some sugar!'

Rose showed no fear. Instead, she smiled and said, 'Come to me, dear. I am sweetness indeed.'

As Pudge approached, then, she raised her hands—and with the long soft roots that grew from her fingers, she began to caress the potato. She tossed thin roots over the shoulders and down the back; she ran ropes of roots around the stubby arms.

She had just begun to tangle Pudge in a net of tender knots when Thistle, seeing the monster so close to her sister, screamed: 'Rosy, Rosy, what are you doing?'

Rose turned and shouted, 'Shut up!'

And in that instant, Pudge shook free. He roared, 'DESSERT!' and swallowed the beautiful Rose all in a single gulp.

Six were four, and four but two, and two no more than one.

Poor Thistle, the youngest of them all, was left alone in the potato house, crying.

'Thistle, Thistle,' she said to herself, 'can you do nothing but cry? No, nothing but cry,' she said.

The tears fell down like rain. Her sighs were like wind in the house.

'Oh, I wish I were tall,' she said. But she was short.

'I wish I were strong.' But she was weak.

'And how I wish I were beautiful.' But she was as plain as a window weed, nothing of value, nothing to use in the fight against Pudge, nothing, no, nothing but tears.

Thistle stumbled from the house. She wandered into the world with neither a thought nor a plan. She had nowhere to go. All the world was lonely now. Potato fields were flat and empty. The sky was cold and grey. And Thistle was missing everybody.

She walked and walked, crying out loud and naming the names of her family: 'Pine, I miss you!' she sobbed. 'Oak, my big brother! Rosy, Rosy, pretty Rose.'

Just then she heard a horrible croaking, like a warty toad speaking. 'I am acquainted with those,' it said. 'Rose and Oak and Pine…'

Thistle rubbed the tears from her eyes and looked, and there on a stump was an ancient bunch-backed Beldame, as old as stone and ugly.

'Really?' the child whispered. 'Did you know them too?'

'Very well indeed,' the Beldame croaked.

Thistle went right over to her and put her chubby hand on the old woman's foot. 'Oh, thank you,' she cried. 'They were my family, my brothers and sister.'

'Aye,' the Beldame hissed with narrow eyes, 'I met them each by each, and each by each I sent them home again.'

'Oh, Mother!' Thistle burst into fresh tears. 'But they

aren't home any more! Pudge has eaten all the height and strength and beauty in the world. What is left? What is left?'

'Little and nothing,' quoth the Beldame, switching ten inches of chin in the air, 'except that I may give thee something worthless to thee, but it pleasures me to give it.'

Thistle sobbed, 'Well, someone should have pleasure in this sad world.'

The Beldame opened her eyes and stared at the child. 'What?' she said. 'Thou wilt take my worthless thing?'

'Yes.'

'Aiee!' cried the Beldame. 'And dost not ask first what I mean to give thee?'

Thistle shook her head. 'You knew my sister and my dear brothers. You comfort me, Mother. I will comfort you.'

'Child,' breathed the ancient Beldame, 'let me kiss thee.'

Thistle nodded, sobbing, still sobbing. 'Kiss me.'

So then the Beldame slid down from her trunk and reached out crooked arms toward Thistle and kissed her. Not one kiss. Not five or ten: she kissed the child a thousand times. Every tear that Thistle shed, the Beldame kissed it.

And every tear, when it was kissed, turned into a thorn.

Soon Thistle was covered by tiny thorns, stem and leaf, hair and blossom, cheek and knee and all ten toes. And the ancient Beldame smiled a very glad smile and whispered, 'Done.'

Then she sang a little song:

> 'Cap-a-pie and foot to brow,
> One child is weaponed now.'

She turned back to her stump. And then, just before she entered it and disappeared, she sighed and said, 'Wee Thistle, thou hast blown the chill from mine old and hoary heart. As for you, lass, go home again. Wait thee there for Pudge, and we shall see what we shall see.'

Thistle. Dear Thistle, with nothing else before her, did go home again.

In the very same place where Pine stood tall and Oak made muscles and Rose tried to charm the monster, Thistle came and waited, facing the door of the potato house, thinking nothing.

BOOM! Exactly at noon the door flew open.

'MY NAME IS PUDGE!' Pudge thundered into the house.

Thistle nodded. 'I know,' she said.

'I'M HUNGRY! HUNGRY! AND READY TO EAT!'

'Yes,' said Thistle. 'I thought so.'

'AND, PORRIDGE,' Pudge roared louder than ever before, 'I'M GOING TO EAT YOU!'

'Yes,' said Thistle. 'Yes.'

The bloated potato began to thump forward on stubby legs. Thistle sighed and bowed her head. A thousand eyes rolled all around her. An enormous mouth gaped wide above her. And then she was swallowed into the gullet of the huge potato.

But this time Pudge did not turn and stomp away.

Instead, the potato's eyes started to blink and to shed tears.

'Mmmmmm!' The potato's thick arms began to beat on the stomach, and Pudge was groaning in terrible pain:

'Mmmmmm! Mmmmmmmm-ahhh!'

For the thorns of Thistle were stinging Pudge on the inside, in all the tender places.

'WHAT DID I EAT?' Pudge bellowed, falling down to the floor. 'AND WHAT IS EATING ME?'

The burning of a thousand thorns grew hotter and hotter inside the potato, huger and huger—till Pudge the potato burst at the middle, exploding all over the house.

And out of the hole came the good man, Thistle's papa, sticky with mashed potatoes, but healthy and grinning. And out came the good woman, too!

Next, Pine jumped out, a little bit bent. And Oak, somewhat weak and woozy. But both were alive and smiling.

Rose appeared, smiling too, though the bloom had gone out of her cheek a bit. Soon everyone was looking at the hole in Pudge. A father, a mother, two brothers and a sister were holding their breath and waiting, waiting...

Then out crept Thistle, and the whole family shouted and started to laugh!

'Thistle! Thistle!' they sang, as if her name were a song. They formed a ring and danced around her.

Yes, she was still short and chubby and plain; but all of her thorns had turned into dimples. And dimples are lovely, dimples are things that people love to touch. So her sister and brothers and mother and father touched and hugged her very much.

'Oh, Thistle! You could do nothing but cry—but tears were the best weapons after all!'

So then six were six, together again. And all who lived in the potato house were happy indeed.

And Pudge? Well, of Pudge they made potato soup.

Riding the Horse Whose Name is I AM

*L*ong, long ago, there was an Indian woman who fell in love with a black stallion. She grew so sick with love for this horse, that she said she would die if she could not own him and ride him.

It happened this way.

Early one morning, the woman was standing at the edge of a long, low cliff. The sun was rising behind her, so the cliff made a shadow in the valley at her feet, and on the top of that shadow, like a single feather on the earth, stood her own.

She had stopped to watch a red cloud running south along the western horizon. It was a dust cloud, burning in the early sunlight, and it was going very fast.

She thought, *What can run with such wonderful speed?*

Then she saw a fleet, black creature at the point of the cloud. *A horse!* she whispered. She grinned. She had never seen a horse gallop so fast. It took her breath away. *A pure black and shining stallion*, she said.

Slowly the stallion turned eastward, in the direction of the Indian woman. He had a mane like black flames and a tail that streaked dark smoke behind him. Sometimes he pulled short and leaped into the air, shaking his great head and striking the earth with mighty hooves for the pure pleasure of the impact; but then he thrust his head forward and broke into that low, level, thundering gallop, as swift as a summer storm cloud coming.

He's looking at me! the woman gasped. She covered her

mouth with two hands and opened her eyes very wide. *That black stallion is looking—and coming straight to me!*

The woman had no husband. Shortly after their little boy was born, her husband had left to fight a distant battle and had never returned. While he was still alive the people of their village said, 'Look at Winona. Do you see? She loves him so much that her eyes go green with the loving.'

It was true. When the woman named Winona loved someone truly, she would laugh and her dark eyes flashed a deep green fire. But her son was ten years old now. In the ten years since her husband disappeared no one had seen the green light in her eyes—

—until this very moment.

For the thunder of the stallion's hooves caused an equal drumming in the woman's heart. The closer he came, the more she grinned, and soon she was giggling with excitement.

Then he drew up and stopped, right where her shadow lay on the ground.

The woman whispered, 'Horse, you are so beautiful!'

The stallion said, *Yes.* The stallion nickered within his enormous chest, and it seemed to Winona that he said *Yes* to her, so she began to pant in the nearness of the magnificent being.

Suddenly the black horse rose rampant and stroked the air with his forelegs, gazing still into the woman's eyes. Their faces were dead level together. It was as if they spoke, but wordlessly. She scarcely knew what they were saying together.

Then down he came. His hooves hit the earth and her shadow, just in the region of her chest, and she burst out laughing. She couldn't help it. That word had been both mute and wonderful.

Again the stallion rose up, and again he stamped the shadow where her heart was. So sweet was the feeling in her that she said, 'Horse, I love you! I love you!'

And her eyes fairly flashed with a marvellous green light.

For the third time the black stallion stood on two legs and nodded his great head and then spoke by the planting of his forehooves upon her shadow, and she cried out, and she said, 'What is your name?'

But the stallion had already turned from the cliff toward the wide horizon and was galloping with such speed and freedom that he seemed not to touch the earth. He looked like a rushing black cloud and fire only. But he whinnied as he went, and it seemed to the woman that he said, *I will be what I will be!* Like lightning he boomed, *I am what I am! That is my name.* And he was gone.

In the village that day the people said, 'Look at Winona! Look at her eyes! She has found someone to love again.'

She knelt down in front of her son, and she hugged him, and she said, 'Would you like to fly as fast as the wind? Would you like to shout with the sound of a thundercloud and cross valleys side to side in one long bound? *Hokshila*, there is a horse who, if you ride him, can make you as swift and as strong as *Wakinyan*, the thunder beings!'

The woman began to ask everywhere in the village

whether anyone knew of the stallion whose name was *I AM*, who was as black as night and as bright as fire.

But no one had ever heard of such a horse.

So she went to the wise woman who lived in the cave of a high mountain, Winyan, so old and wrinkled that her face looked very angry, like the frowning mountain itself.

The Indian woman named Winona said, 'Do you know of the black stallion who runs the plains free and alone, who is beautiful, whose name is *I AM*?'

Winyan sat in front of the cave with her old legs straight in front of her. 'Why?' she said.

Winona said, 'Because I wish to know the cost of him. I want to own him.'

Winyan said, 'Why?'

Winona said, 'Because I want him for my horse. I want to ride him.'

Winyan said, 'Why?'

Winona paused a moment and dropped her eyes. She was blushing under the fierce gaze of this old woman. She said, 'Because I love him.'

'You love him,' said Winyan.

'Yes.'

'How much do you love him?'

Winona looked up. She looked directly into the bright, tiny eyes of the ancient Winyan, and she said, 'With all my heart. Yes, and with all my soul and with all my might.'

So Winyan said, 'Then that is how much the black stallion will cost. For you to ride that stallion, it will cost you everything you have.'

'I can do that?' cried the Indian woman. 'Yes, I can surely do that!'

She ran back to the village in joy and in great haste, laughing as she went.

Then she gathered together everything that she had. Clothing, tools, the buffalo-horn knife which had been her husband's, her bedding, her precious quill-worked moccasins, the two sway-backed ponies which she and her son used for transport, everything.

The boy watched his mother and laughed with her. He was glad that she was so happy; but he didn't understand it. When she began to sell all their possessions, then, he said, 'Why are you doing this?'

She said, '*Hokshila*, it is worth it! Such goodness is about to come into our lives! We will have a horse to carry us, a stallion stronger and more beautiful than any creature you have ever seen, and then there will be no need of this stuff, no!'

So she sold it all, and climbed the craggy mountain again to Winyan, and laid before that ancient woman all the treasure she had gained.

It made a nice, small heap on the ground.

'There,' said Winona. 'There is everything I have. Now let me purchase the stallion that I might own him and ride him.'

Her eyes flashed the deep green light of excitement and sweet love. She could hardly sit still.

Winyan stared a while at the younger woman, piercing her with a fierce gaze. Finally she said, 'How much do you love this horse who is wild, who runs alone, whose name is *I AM*?'

Winona smiled and blinked. 'I told you,' she said. 'I love him with all my heart and soul and might.'

'And how much did I say such a horse and such a love would cost you?'

'Everything I have,' said Winona. 'And this is everything. There is no more.'

The old woman said, 'What is in your hand?'

The young woman opened both hands. 'They are empty,' she said. 'There is nothing in my hand.'

'No,' said Winyan sharply, frowning as hard as the mountain, 'but what is *in* your hand? In*side* your hand?'

'Oh,' said Winona. 'You mean what I can do.'

'For you to ride that stallion, it will cost you everything that you have. Everything.'

The Indian woman understood: everything both outside herself and inside herself. Also her skills and talents, which were her things too. Yes, yes. Love goes very deep. And her love was as much inside herself as outside where people could see it. Yes, everything: she could surely do that.

So she walked back to the village, thinking about the task to come.

First she went to her son and hugged him.

'*Hokshila*,' she said, 'you must stay a while with your uncle. I have a hard job to do. I can't look after you for a while. But when I come back,' she said, 'we will laugh together, you and I. We will mount the wind and all the world will say, "They have found a treasure of the greatest value." When I come back, *hokshila*, we will be so glad together!'

Then the woman went to work. She worked with her

hands and her teeth. She flattened porcupine quills by biting them between her front teeth; then she dyed them bright colours; then she wove them into shirts and dresses and moccasins, creating pictures of such beauty that the people of the village marvelled at her skill.

She made pictures of a smoky stallion, a being whose eyes looked straight back at all who viewed the artwork. Moreover, the horse seemed to be breathing. Some people felt afraid, because the horse was wild and wilful and looked as if he might leap from the picture into the world.

All day and all night Winona worked. No sleep for her. Only the barest minimum of food and water. Her teeth were worn down to the gums with chewing. Her fingers bled continually. She exhausted herself. She emptied herself. She exchanged her talent and her might and her strength for a little treasure and this, finally, she carried back to the mountain, up to the cave, where she poured it upon the first heap. And then she sat down very tired.

Winyan crouched there, staring at her. Winyan waited, saying nothing.

So Winona said, 'There. This time I have brought you everything that I have. Now, then, let me buy the black stallion. Let me grow light and limber and strong again by riding him.'

Ancient Winyan was silent. The old woman, whose eye was as sharp as thorns, whose face was as broken as stone, whose legs stuck out like sticks in front of her, said nothing. She just stared and then, slowly, she began to shake her head.

'What?' said the poor Winona. 'What? This is all! Look at my hands. They are empty. They are so empty that they are bloody. My strength is all dried up. There is nothing left. Nothing! This heap is everything that I have.'

Still, the old woman kept shaking her head—sadly, as it seemed to Winona. Sadly.

'What else is there?' she begged.

And Winyan said, 'When you go back to the village, is there nothing of value that shall come out to meet you and to greet you?'

It was then that the Indian woman named Winona began to cry, for she understood. She cried and she could not stop crying.

Winyan said, 'How much do you love the horse?'

And that is how much she loved the horse.

She walked, weeping, back to the village. She went to the uncle of her son and told him that he must be the boy's father now, for she could not be his mother any more. No, she could not, because he could no longer be her son. She must have no children, nor any who loved her in such a manner as to be a richness and a treasure to her. She begged a little gift in return for her child.

The man went into the tipi for the small payment.

When he came out, the boy followed.

The boy said, 'Mama, what are you doing? Why are you doing this?' He, too, started to cry, just as she was crying.

But she didn't answer him.

She took the tiny payment and turned and walked away, wailing and lamenting as she went.

Then she laid this bit upon the heap of her earlier offerings.

She raised her sad eyes and said, 'There. Surely that is all I have. There is no more that I can give.'

Ancient Winyan now seemed no larger than a doll carved in cherry wood, and her eyes were charred with watching the world so long. She sat still. She did not move even so much as to shake her head. She only stared at Winona.

Winona whispered, 'Even this? This is not enough?'

It seemed to Winona that the old woman, too, allowed a little water to run down her cheek.

Therefore, she said, 'Not enough. But what else can there be?'

Slowly Winyan rose to her feet. Painfully she stepped to the younger woman. She kissed her forehead, then stepped back and looked again in silence.

'Me,' said Winona.

Winyan nodded.

'You mean me. I am also to be payment. It costs me, myself, my life.'

Winyan ceased nodding, because this was the truth. This finally was the whole of the truth.

Winona bowed her head. She said softly, 'I love the black and beautiful horse. I love him with all my heart, and with all my soul, and with all my might. But,' she said, and she looked up at the tiny grandmother, 'but there is a problem, Winyan.'

She had stopped crying now. Winona spoke like a child, both humble and puzzled. 'If someone must pay her very self for the stallion, then who is there to ride him? If I am spent, how can he carry me?

'Winyan?' she whispered, 'If I no longer am, how can I be his rider?'

Softly, softly, more softly than stones when they speak in the moonlight, the ancient woman said, *Well, we will see what we will see.*

One evening an Indian youth was standing at the edge of a long, low cliff. The descending sun was in his eyes, a great red ball that made him squint as he peered westward.

Something had caught his attention on the horizon, something of such intensity that it seemed to black the lower part of the sun and to cause deep trembling in the earth itself.

He thought, *What can move with such power? What shakes the ground with its tread?*

His eyes adjusted, and he saw even in the enormous sun the form of a horse. *Oiyaaa!* he breathed with admiration. That horse must be marvellous, huge, a sun-walker!

Then he saw that the steed was making a wide turn eastward; so a horse seemed to be stepping out of the sun and onto the plains. Then the stallion was galloping in his direction. This was not a seeming nor a vision: though wild horses avoid humans and must be chased and caught, this one was running straight toward the young Indian on the cliff.

Ah, what a beautiful black mount it could make! It dashed the air. It seemed to ignite the air, so fast did it move. It tore the air as lightning tears the sky. The young man began to laugh in delight for what he was watching. He shouted and whooped, and the horse likewise raised its head and shook its fiery mane and whinnied as if laughing along.

And this was very remarkable, for the lad had not laughed in five years. When he was younger his mother could make him laugh. Her swift affections, her marvellous moods always lifted him heart and soul, and as long as she was near he was happy. But five years ago she disappeared and he stopped laughing—

—until now.

For the shock of this stallion, suddenly galloping straight for him as if the horse were chasing the man, was exactly like the rich surprise his mother once had been.

And then the young man realized that the horse was also looking at him. Even as it came closer—slowing to a canter, slowing to a walk—the beautiful black horse was gazing directly into his eyes. He tingled all over, so to be seen.

But then the stallion was standing not ten feet away, and the boy began to cry. He couldn't help it. He went down on his knees, weeping. And the horse stepped forward, bowing and nickering, then lifting a soft snout and nudging his face.

The eyes that gazed at the Indian lad—they were green.

The horse's eyes, all filled with love for the one whom they looked upon, burned with a deep green light.

'Mama,' the Indian said, burying his face in the horse's neck. 'Oh, mama!'

That night it seemed to thunder.

People looked out of their lodges, expecting rain. Instead,

they saw a white moon and a black sky filled with stars. They heard the sound of a rushing wind, but they felt nothing.

Then, suddenly—crossing the sky at the tops of the trees with lightning for feet—they saw a black horse blotting the stars, and on its back a young man riding. The moonlight lit his face like silver.

And the people said, 'Isn't that the young man from our village—the son of Winona? How did he learn to ride the wind?'